John F Plimmer's

The Victorian Detective's Case Review

A thrilling novel – The first in a series of Case Reviews conducted by Inspector Rayner of Scotland Yard

To Phil Thomas
with whom I have the honour of
calling a true friend and former
colleague and his lovely wife, Rosemary

Chapter One

During the mid-nineteenth century many regions throughout the United Kingdom were notoriously known for their poverty, violence and crime. One of the most infamous districts was London's Whitechapel, a conglomeration of narrow passageways, courtyards, squares and enclosed alleyways, in which its inhabitants struggled to survive on a daily basis.

Life was cheap in the backstreets where danger lurked on every corner during the hours of darkness. Fatal diseases such as Cholera and Typhoid played their part in threatening the existence of human life. And yet, when news of a murder most foul reached the ears of the populace, fear and condemnation spread like wildfire, usually resulting in public demands for the killer to be quickly brought to justice.

So it was, during the winter of 1860 when two elderly sisters, residing alone and making a scant living from their Tripe Shop near to the centre of Whitechapel, were found brutally murdered in their home. A hue and cry followed and the London newspapers accused Scotland Yard of being inept and inefficient, as the initial Investigation failed to identify the culprit.

Finally, as the days turned into weeks and the weeks into months without any positive action being taken by police, the public disquiet diluted. The notoriety which had clung to the high-profile atrocity was quickly forgotten and the double murder remained on Scotland Yard's files as being undetected.

When Inspector Richard Rayner and his Sergeant, Henry Bustle, apprehensively stepped into the Superintendent's office, it was similar to landing in the middle of rolling mists clinging to wild moorland. The detectives could vaguely see their senior officer through a thick haze of swirling tobacco smoke being pumped out of the Head of the Detective Branch's favourite pipe.

"You are late inspector," was the hostile greeting, which penetrated through the visual obstruction, indicating the location of Frederick Morgan; sitting behind a large oak desk and facing the door.

Rayner paused to glance at his pocket watch before proffering some mitigation in answer to the accusation.

"Only by a couple of minutes, sir. Have you seen the weather outside?"

"What the bleedin' hell as that got to do with a lack of punctuality? We have a little snow and the whole city seems to come to a standstill, providing people such as yourself with an excuse for blatant inefficiency," was the sarcastic riposte.

The Superintendent was a forty-year old Welshman from Porthcawl, and a former Major in the Coldstream Guards, whose regimented way of life had never left him since leaving the military. In fact, those who worked under Frederick Morgan, suspected their most senior detective continued working under the pretext of retaining his Army rank. However, although stern and acutely disciplined in his approach to man management, almost to a frustrating level of rigidity, the man in charge of the Detective Branch at Scotland Yard was also regarded by most as being utterly fair and without bias.

Morgan was a lifelong devoted bachelor, who resided in a privately-owned property in Manning Street, Bermondsey. He spent most of his time though at the Metropolitan Police Headquarters, where he held the position as Head of the Detective Branch. Whilst not being totally opposed to the female sex, the Head of the Detective Branch stringently believed that women created too many diversions for a man holding down such a privileged and prestigious situation.

He stood in his usual straight-backed posture, gazing for a moment out of the large window behind his desk, taking stock of the worsening outside weather conditions. The slight flurries of snow had now turned into a continuous fall of golf balls. Heavy drifts were now apparent, and except for the odd horse and carriage struggling to gain some purchase on the cobbled stones below Morgan's window, the streets appeared to have become deserted.

The temperature had also dropped quite noticeably and the Superintendent stepped around his desk. Ignoring his two visitors, he opened the door to his office and shouted down the outside corridor for a junior rank to put more coal on his fire.

"I understand you require us to look into a fifteen-year old murder sir," Richard Rayner enquired, as Morgan returned to his chair, after closing the door behind him.

The senior officer remained momentarily silent, preferring to re-ignite his briar, which resulted in more clouds of blue smoke spiraling up towards the ceiling. He then sat back to languidly relax and enjoy the taste of the same tobacco, which was creating such an obnoxious smell in the room. Finally, his watery eyes fell once again on the Inspector, and he quietly admitted that for once the newspapers had got it right.

"It's the fifteenth anniversary of the brutal murders of the two elderly sisters who used to keep the Tripe Shop in Mount Street, at the corner with Turner Street, near to the London Hospital."

"Emily and Gertrude Barratt," Rayner remarked, confirming that he too, had a good memory, "I recall the incident, and the public furore that followed. I had only been a beat man for a couple of months when it happened."

"They were both bludgeoned to death, but we never managed to arrest the killer. And yes, it took a long time before the hue and cry died down, but now gentlemen, the crime has come back to haunt us with the newspapers throwing all kinds of accusations our way."

"I see."

"No, you don't see Inspector. The Commissioner is pulling his whiskers out over this, and is demanding that I re-open the case and give it to you, in the faint hope of finding the homicidal jackal who was responsible."

It was not the first historic case given to Richard Rayner to investigate. The tall, dark haired and handsome, thirty-one year old Detective Inspector, had frequently displayed an uncanny talent for detecting long forgotten crimes. Those once notorious atrocities which had remained collecting dust, shelved and labeled as being undetected. In recent years he had accomplished a great deal of success, which had earned him a reputation for being one of the top detective's at Scotland Yard.

The immaculately dressed officer had previously graduated from Christchurch College, Oxford, with a degree in Mathematics. That part of his young life had been followed by a period of employment as a lecturer, before seeking a more adventurous and rewarding life. Hence the reason the academic had joined the Metropolitan Police before becoming a central figure in its newly formed Detective Department. He was what some would regard as a 'natty' dresser, always remaining smartly presented in his daily attire, in contrast to the appearance of his loyal Detective Sergeant.

Henry Bustle was, unlike Richard Rayner, a married man who had far greater responsibilities in the form of a wife, Nelly, and their four young children. The Sergeant's priority was to clothe and feed his family, before indulging in any personal benefits. His preference was to spend what little money was left over from running his household, on more practical, if usually plain and drab items of clothing.

Morgan placed a finger down the starched collar that adorned his neck, to ease an itching sensation he was experiencing. He reached down to pick up a file of papers from the floor, before placing them on the top of his desk. It was his habit to go through a fairly frequent ritual of flicking imaginary pieces of fluff from the shoulders of his jacket, which he did before declaring, "This is what we have left of the original Investigation, so I suggest you waste no more time, and quickly acquaint yourselves with every minute detail."

Rayner nodded at his Sergeant, who took hold of the file and nervously tucked them under his arm. Unlike his Inspector, Henry Bustle had never been comfortable in Morgan's presence. As much as Richard Rayner had tried to convince his colleague that the Superintendent's bark was greater than his bite, the Sergeant could never be convinced.

Again, unlike his Inspector, Bustle hadn't received anything close to an easy upbringing, working from a young age in the butchering industry. He was much shorter in height to Rayner, but stockier and with a scar running down one side of his face, which changed colour according to the temperature outside. He viewed the disfigurement as a trophy proudly displayed from a street altercation fought many years previously. Although destined to remain a butcher for the rest of his working days, Bustle had become restless with a burning desire to improve his lot. He possessed sufficient motivation towards self-education and eventually sought, what he believed would be a more rewarding life, as a member of the Metropolitan Police.

"Might I ask what you remember of the case, sir?" the Inspector asked.

The Superintendent stood from his chair, and removed his pipe from his mouth, before loudly claiming, "I remember nothing Inspector, because at the time I was fighting the Ruskies at Sevastopol as one of Her Majesty's Majors in the Coldstream Guards."

"I never knew you were in the Crimea, Superintendent," Henry Bustle whimpered.

"Good God man. Well you bloody well know now," the Welshman bawled back, "Now be off and Rayner, I want this one brought to a successful conclusion as quickly as possible. As the Commissioner frequently reminds me, the reputation of the Department is at stake."

"We shall do our very best Superintendent."

As both men turned to leave, the door opened and a young constable, Jack Robinson, stepped into the office, carrying a heavy bucket of coal. The blue tinge on his facial features confirmed the junior rank had recently been exposed to the outside frosty air, obviously having visited the coal shed in the back yard.

"Wait," Morgan called to the Inspector and Sergeant, "I am seconding young Robinson here to work with you, to give what assistance he can to help you with this one. After he's built up my fire, of course."

Rayner wasn't completely convinced of the real reason why such a young inexperienced officer was being afforded the experience of working with himself and Henry Bustle. But that wasn't the time to question the decision. The Inspector just nodded, before suggesting to the young constable he joined them in his office, after depositing more coal on the Superintendent's fire.

The lad was overjoyed and the look of appreciation on his face reminded Rayner of a man who had just been introduced to Royalty.

Before becoming the victims of cold bloodied murder, both Gertrude Barratt and her spinster sister, Emily, had lived at the back of their small shop. The premises were within sight of the London Hospital, an institution built for the specific purpose of administering to the impoverished people of Whitechapel. From the front of the small establishment, the two elderly ladies sold various types of cooked offal to the local residents. They were popular with the local people, occasionally being known to give their produce away to those found to be in dire circumstances, and deprived of having sufficient funds to feed their families.

Each evening, after closing their shop for the day, one of the sisters would visit the neighbours who lived next door, Thomas Braithwaite and his wife Lillian. A steaming hot bowl of Tripe and Onions would be handed over, which helped to sustain a close friendship between the Barratt sisters and their immediate neighbours.

That was until one particular winter's evening, when neither of the sisters appeared on the Braithwaites' doorstep. In response, Lillian decided to make sure all was well with the two elderly ladies, and made her way to the front door of the shop, which she found to be closed and bolted from the inside.

Before returning to her own habitat, the inquisitive woman overheard voices coming from inside Gertrude and Emily Barratt's dwelling, one of which belonged to a man. Believing the sisters had a visitor, she thought nothing more of it and returned home.

It was during the early hours of the following morning, that Lillian thought she heard a loud bang coming from the shop next door, which was accompanied by a female's cry for help. Unable to awaken her snoring husband Thomas, and dressed only in her nightclothes with a shawl wrapped around her shoulders, Mrs. Braithwaite once again left the comfort of her house. She tentatively stepped through a small gate, which led to the long, narrow garden at the back of her neighbours residence.

A heavy frost had fallen, and she noticed the outline of footsteps leading up the garden, and coming from the back door of the kitchen, adjacent to the parlour at the rear of the shop. There was a dim light coming from a lantern inside the backroom, and upon peering through an opening in the drawn curtains Lillian was taken aback by the grotesque sight of murder most foul. Both women could be seen in the dimness of the interior. Emily Barratt was spread eagled across a well-worn floor mat, and her sister Gertrude, collapsed in a large soft chair just on the other side of the window. Both victims were covered in blood, and it was obvious they were both dead.

A frantic and distressed Lillian wasted little time in running to fetch her husband, but was fortunate to see an all-night cabbie coming along the street from the direction of the main gates of the hospital. She flagged the horse and carriage down and described to the driver the scene she had just had the misfortune of seeing.

The cabbie immediately elected to fetch the local police, and within a few minutes the Investigation into the double murders had commenced.

When news of the brutal killings spread, there was an overwhelming public response, resulting in vigilante groups patrolling the streets in response to an initial lack of success in catching the killer. A number of incidents followed whereby suspects were stoned and seriously injured. Windows of houses were smashed, where individuals who had been interviewed as suspects by investigating officers, resided. Eventually, as time passed by the tension within the community eased and the number of violent episodes subsided. Normality in people's daily routines was quickly restored, although the person responsible for the brutal killings remained at large.

The two detectives were still mulling through the initial reports when Constable Jack Robinson appeared in Richard Rayner's office, which was just down the corridor from the Superintendent's.

"Put the kettle on Jack," Bustle immediately directed.

"Later," Rayner counter commanded, "I want you to sit in with us Jack, and become as acquainted as we are with the details of the case."

The tall, lanky young man with a pale face beneath a mop of unruly dark brown hair, and the makings of a thin moustache across the top of his upper lip, held only one ambition. He had always wanted to be a detective. Brimming with enthusiasm, Robinson immediately pulled up a chair, to sit at the side of the Detective Sergeant.

Henry Bustle scowled at the newcomer, before acknowledging to himself some of his Detective Inspector's character traits. Richard Rayner would have been determined to give the youngster as much opportunity to become involved in the Investigation as was possible. He was well aware that Rayner was that kind of man.

"I see from the Post Mortem report Henry, the cause of death was due to a fractured skull to both victims, but according to the Pathologist, a Doctor Scott, there was bruising around Emily Barratt's neck," the leading detective observed.

"Strangulation, before clubbing the woman over the back of the head," Bustle suggested.

"It would appear so, but what does that tell you about the killer?"

Rayner looked directly at Robinson, obviously requiring an opinion.

After quickly giving the circumstances some thought, the young sentient officer declared, "It was a frenzied attack sir, and something said or done had caused the killer to lose his self-control."

"Henry?"

"The perpetrator attacked the woman, before deciding to kill them both, by bludgeoning them to death," the Detective Sergeant opinionated, "Which tells us there must have been some sort of argument between the sisters and their killer, before the murders were committed."

"Exactly, so it does appear that the crimes were not pre-planned, and rather the result of some instantaneous reaction. It also seems evident from what I have read so far, that the reason why the investigating officers found some difficulty in tracking down the killer was a distinct lack of any known motive."

"It seems that way," Bustle agreed, "Nothing was stolen from the house or shop, but I see that one of the constables in attendance, found an unusual button on the floor of the kitchen at the back of the house."

"Where is that reported Henry?" Rayner asked.

"On the third page of Inspector Albert Greening's report sir. He mentions a brass button with an unusual insignia embossed on it; that of a ship's anchor with the name of the Queen beneath it."

"I also see from these papers, that a piece of muslin was recovered inside the shop part of the premises, bearing a label of a supplier by the name of Walker's Offal of Smithfield Market. It seems that the same company supplied washed tripe to the sisters just prior to the murders."

Jack Robinson looked confused and enquired, "How do we know that, Inspector?"

"Because the cloth was found in a small bucket inside the shop, and according to these reports, both the shop and living accommodation were kept spotlessly clean. Therefore, the last delivery the sisters received must have been recent, as they hadn't had an opportunity to dispose of the muslin."

"Why is the absence of any motive important?" the younger member of the trio asked, demonstrating his genuine interest.

"You need to listen more lad," Bustle suggested, "And to talk less."

Rayner smiled at the Sergeant's rebuke of the younger man, and continued to explain, "A motive to a crime enables us to decide which lines of inquiry we will make Jack. When such a motive for murder is not apparent, then the subsequent Investigation usually progresses in the dark, the enquiries therefore having to be made in a sort of ad hoc manner."

Rayner then sat back with both hands resting on top of his desk, before suggesting what he believed those initial lines of enquiry should be, following a delay of fifteen years.

"Jack, I want you to see if the company in Smithfield Market is still in existence, and if so, have they still records of whoever made the deliveries to the sisters' shop on that fateful day in 1860. They might not have any written record, but because of the nature of the incident someone might remember."

The young constable nodded his understanding enthusiastically, and scribbled down a written record of the Inspector's request in his note book.

"Henry, although it's been fifteen years since the murders took place, I still think it would be a good idea to revisit the scene."

"I wonder who owns the shop now?" Bustle queried.

"We shall soon find out."

Rayner smiled confidently, and stepped across the room to retrieve his top hat and frock overcoat. Whether their first day working on the case would bring some success or not, it would be extremely cold once they left the confines of Scotland Yard.

Chapter Two

It was still snowing persistently by the time the two detectives left the warmth and comfort of their headquarters building, heading for Turner Street, Whitechapel. Those few people who could be seen scurrying about, did so with their heads bowed down against the natural phenomenon that had so quickly thrown a thick white blanket over the city.

The cabbie's horse struggled to negotiate the snow-covered cobbled streets, and through sheer perseverance, finally reached Whitechapel Road, until it could progress no further. A snowdrift completely blocked the entire thoroughfare, and the horse stood motionless with both front legs buried in the obstruction, and its head swinging to and fro in sheer confusion.

The driver immediately leapt down, and after offering some reassurance to the animal, opened the carriage door.

"I'm sorry gents, but this is the end of the journey," the cabbie explained, disappointingly, "Old George there can't go any further in this damned weather," he said, referring to his labouring horse.

"Very well cabbie," Rayner answered sympathetically, "It can't be helped. How far is it before we reach Turner Street?"

"Just a couple of hundred yards down on the right sir, just before you reach the hospital. Mount Street is just a short-ways down from there."

The Inspector paid what fare was owed to the man, and began to walk attentively with Henry Bustle at his side, and both men finding it difficult to keep their feet. After trudging a short distance, the Sergeant looked back to see the cabbie still trying to back his horse away from the wall of snow that had prematurely ended their journey.

"This is no place for sensible men, Inspector," the Sergeant claimed, "I should be at home now with Nellie and the four kids, helping to stoke up the fire."

"You are always complaining Henry, mostly about the tedium of police work. And yet, here is another opportunity to examine a crime scene at first hand, which is of the utmost importance and certainly not tedious."

"A crime scene of some fifteen years ago," the Sergeant quickly qualified, the bitter cold now beginning to infiltrate through his woolen cloak.

"We should be coming up to Mount Street shortly," Rayner offered, his eyes filled with enthusiasm, which was in contrast to his colleague.

In the prosaic world of the Metropolitan Police, the Detective Inspector was similar to a shining beacon amongst a sea of apathy. Richard Rayner appeared to meet every challenge with the same high level of drive and motivation. Not once could he ever be accused of portraying the slightest sign of defeatism, even when faced with the most frustrating difficulties or circumstances surrounding an Investigation. Even when entering a new domain, particularly where others feared to tread, he advanced with the same edacious hunger for knowledge, which would assist in solving a problem.

Whitechapel was overcrowded mostly with Jewish and Irish immigrants at that time, and was recognised by most as being one of the poorest areas in London. Those who lived in the East End suffered from not just overcrowding, but also starvation and the absence of anything close to being reasonable living conditions. It naturally followed therefore that crime was rife throughout the district, encouraging a vast number of brothels in competition with each other. Low class prostitutes openly spent most of their nights walking the streets, no matter how inclement the weather, or freezing cold the conditions happened to be. It was the only way the majority of ladies of the night, knew how to obtain sufficient funds required to survive for another twenty-four hours. Especially when for some of them, nourishment could only come from a gin bottle.

Knowing only too well the destitution that gripped Whitechapel, Richard Rayner considered one possibility. The Inspector wondered whether it had been possible that one of those street girls had actually come across the man they were now hunting, on the same night of the sisters' gruesome murders. He also gave thought to how many, if any, had been interviewed during the initial stages of the Investigation, with that possibility in mind. The Inspector had previously received the kind of help from prostitutes that had assisted the progression of a number of complex cases. He vehemently believed the majority of girls would willingly help, provided they were treated with dignity and respect. Albert Greening, the officer in charge at the time, would be able to provide that information for him, and it was imperative that the former Inspector was seen at the first opportunity.

The detectives stopped, after noticing a small line of mothers with their children, all standing in the freezing conditions, by a canvas tent which had steam pouring out from the interior.

"They save peoples' lives, Henry," Rayner remarked.

"Lord only knows where we would be without soup kitchens," the Sergeant quickly replied, "Those kids are not much older than my youngest."

Most of the Christian 'Food Shops' introduced across the East End to help support the starving, had been organised by a Nottingham man, William Booth, who became the founder of the Salvation Army and whose first Mission was on Whitechapel Road.

The Inspector shook his head, looking down with disdain at the young frozen blue faces and bare feet, standing there on the snow-covered pavement. The air was filled with the sound of young coughing fits, resulting from various chest infections and other ailments. Both men had seen similar scenes before on many occasions, yet were still moved when witnessing such human depravity at first hand.

"It's no wonder we have so much illness and disease Henry," Rayner remarked with genuine concern.

Although the Sergeant's outward appearance seemed to be made of granite, nothing could cause him greater distress than to see mere infants having to survive in such inhumane conditions, and he felt as if he should lift them all up in his arms and take them home with him. But before he could continue with his cerebration, the two detectives finally reached Turner Street.

At last the snow appeared to be easing, as both men looked across at the complex of the London Hospital, which had a couple of horse drawn carriages standing outside the front gates.

"A hospital built to support the impoverished," Bustle quipped, "But with insufficient food to go around."

"I totally agree Henry, but today we must leave the charitable endeavours to those with big hearts. We have other work to do," Rayner said, as they turned to walk down Turner Street, towards the corner with Mount Street.

It was exactly as the two officers from Scotland Yard had anticipated, the Tripe Shop no longer existed and in its place. stood a small leathery.

Richard Rayner stood for a moment looking up at the premises, before taking in the immediate locality. He asked his Sergeant to wait, before slowly walking down the narrow thoroughfare of Mount Street for a few yards. The Inspector carefully observed the terraced houses and back alleyways on either side. When he returned to the corner, Henry Bustle was stamping his feet on the ground, with both arms tucked into the armpits of his jacket. He was impatient to seek the warmth of the leather shop's interior.

The Inspector led the way through the front door, and immediately detected the strong smell of animal hide. There was shelving attached to a couple of the inner walls, all filled with boots, some repaired, others awaiting attention. Towards the back of the room sat an elderly man with hunched up shoulders. He was blessed with pure white hair and bushy whiskers reaching down each side of his face, and was wearing a tattered grey woolen jumper beneath a sleeveless leather waistcoat. The obvious proprietor was fully engaged in stretching a piece of brown leather between two clamps fixed to each end of a small wooden table.

Standing next to him was a youth with a dirty face, and mop of fair hair that hadn't seen a comb or brush for many a day. The lad stared across at the visitors, as if surprised to see customers at that time of the day.

"How can I help you gentlemen," the old man said in a polite voice, standing from his rickety stool and approaching the counter with a slight look of discomfort on his face. It was noticeable how he walked with one hand pressing against the base of his spine.

Rayner introduced himself and his Sergeant, before confirming they were investigating the murders of the two elderly women, which had taken place all those years before.

The proprietor looked surprised at first, and when the Inspector asked for his name, he answered, "Thomas Fuller sir. I had the good fortune to purchase this property following that dreadful incident, and have been carrying out my business here, ever since."

Fuller then turned and indicated the youth, who he explained was named Albert, and was there to assist the tanner in running errands and making deliveries around the locality.

"Might we impose on you sir," Rayner courteously requested, "To show us your living quarters at the back, where we believe the crimes took place."

The old man bowed his acquiescence and invited the detectives to follow him out the back of the shop.

They found the parlour to be dark, illumined only by the natural light coming through a singular window, which looked out on to the rear garden. There was a two-seater sofa and a leather single chair inside the room, with a small wooden table pressed against the back wall. A single mat commandeered the floorboards at the front of a small hearth, and Rayner asked the obvious question.

"I take it Mr. Fuller, that the furniture has been replaced since you first moved in here?"

"Yes, I replaced everything on the same day as I arrived."

"Including the wallpaper?"

"Yes, of course. The room has been re-decorated twice over the past few years. Can you blame me after what took place here?"

"Not at all sir."

With the occupant's permission, the Inspector then lit a lantern resting on top of the fire place, and immediately began to examine the floorboards, in particular those beneath the mat. He then looked closely at the window frame, which from its age was obviously the same that would have been present when the sisters resided there, but found nothing; there were no jemmy marks or other signs of a forcible entry that might still have remained visible.

"When you first came here, were there any pictures hanging on the walls?" Rayner asked the leather worker.

"There were a few, but I sold them off," he admitted before pausing, "All except one, which I found hanging in the shop. It's a painting of HMS Duke of Wellington and being a mariner in my younger day, I couldn't part with it."

"Have you still got it?"

"Yes, it's upstairs somewhere. I've often thought about bringing it back down, but never seemed to have the opportunity"

"Would you be so kind as to take Sergeant Bustle with you upstairs and try and recover the painting for me?"

"Do you think it's important, Inspector?"

"It's too early to say, sir."

"Very well," the old man agreed, still nursing his sore back with one hand, before making his way out of the parlour, with the Sergeant following at his heels.

Whilst left alone, Richard Rayner stood near the centre of the room, trying to re-enact in his mind what had taken place on that fateful night inside the small Tripe Shop in Mount Street. He recalled the neighbour, Lillian Braithwaite, stating at the time, she had heard a woman cry out for help, and could only imagine the horror the two victims experienced in that same confined parlour.

The kitchen at the very rear of the building would have been similar to when the elderly ladies lived there, and the Inspector again, confirmed there were no signs of any forcible entry having been made.

He stepped outside into the long narrow garden, where the woman from next door had claimed she had seen footprint impressions on the frosty ground, leading from the house towards the small gate at the bottom of the enclosed plot. The garden itself had been neglected, and the path Rayner followed took him to the gate. There was a communal walkway running alongside the backs of the line of houses on one side of Mount Street. Once through the gate, one end of the walkway was blocked by the side of a house which would have fronted Turner Street. That meant if the killer made his escape through the garden area, he would have been forced to turn left once he'd passed through the gate.

The Inspector continued, until he eventually came out half way up Mount Street, just a few yards from the front of what had been the Tripe Shop. From there, the killer could easily have turned left down Mount Street, into Turner Street and disappeared into the mesh of alleyways and narrow side streets of Whitechapel.

By the time Rayner returned to the shop and rear parlour, Henry Bustle was standing next to the elderly occupier, with both men gazing down at an old framed painting of a ship, which had been placed on the sofa.

"Ah, HMS Windsor Castle," the Inspector claimed, seeing a vision of a Royal Naval Ship of the Line, running under both steam and sail."

"You know the ship, Inspector?" Thomas Fuller asked.

"Only from studying Nautical Measurements and Weights, when at

Oxford. This particular vessel carried seventy four guns."

"It records the ship as being HMS Duke of Wellington across the bottom," Henry Bustle quickly pointed out, "And is dated 1853."

"Yes, and by Sir Thomas Craven, a well-known marine artist, but the ship was launched as HMS Windsor Castle, later to be renamed the Duke of Wellington."

"Do you think it might be valuable?" Fuller enquired.

"In all probability, but I am no expert in art, sir," Rayner admitted, taking hold of the picture and turning it so the back was exposed. He then carefully scrutinised the edging around the frame, putting the lantern to good use, until discovering part of the hardboard panel had been removed and clumsily put back together.

The Inspector maneuvered a finger down the inside of the panel until he felt something tucked down inside. Again, using as much care as he possibly could to avoid damaging the frame itself, he managed to grip a folded piece of paper between two fingers. Slowly and cautiously, he extracted the item from its concealment, with both his observers looking on in fascination.

The passage of time had tinted the paper brown, and after placing the mysterious item on top of the small wooden table, Richard Rayner produced a folded knife from the inside pocket of his frock coat. Again, with the utmost care the detective placed the blade in between the folds, and opened up the paper. Revealed on one side was a missive, which was almost illegible. A few lines of handwritten scrawl read:

'To my dearest mother

With love and affection from your loving son Herbert'.

The Inspector then carefully re-folded the note, before sliding it into the inside pocket of his jacket.

"I'm sure you won't mind us keeping this, sir," he said to Thomas Fuller, "And in the meantime, if you decide to sell the painting would you be so kind as to notify us."

"Of course, Inspector."

Rayner then turned to, Bustle and confirmed the obvious.

"It appears to have been a gift from a son to his mother, Henry."

"Yes, but why keep such knowledge hidden behind the picture?"

"That is for us to find out."

"According to the reports, neither of the sister's was ever married."

"That seems to be the case, Henry. We need to call on the man who led the inquiry, Albert Greening. Perhaps he can help us further. It might be of course that the missive was not connected with either of the victims."

"Not a very convincing co-incidence though sir."

Chapter Three

Jack Robinson was no stranger to the hustle and bustle of Smithfield Market, having spent a great deal of his youth helping his father deliver carcasses of sheep, cattle and pigs there, from a local Abattoir. The scene remained the same as he recalled, with a multitude of people treading across ground covered in thick mud and manure. Almost every occupation in the food chain was represented, from farmers, drovers, to butchers, each vociferously proclaiming their individual métier. Pick pockets, cut purses, thieves and other malefactors, were also a constant threatening presence, mingling in and amongst the throngs of business people.

The pigs oinked; the sheep bleated and the cattle steamed, as the young constable maneuvered his way around the interior. He viewed the various fixed billboards above the heads of the various dealers, most of whom were dressed in cow gowns. Finally, he found what had taken him to the market. In one far corner was the legend of 'Walkers Offal' hanging across a wide opening, next to some tall stacks of hay and straw.

As he made off in that direction, determined to extradite the task given him, he failed to notice the muscular figure standing back in the shadows. A pair of alert eyes watched the young constable's every move from a covert position on the perimeter of the market area.

Sitting alone in his office at Scotland Yard, Richard Rayner was busy chalking his own record of the events of that morning on a blackboard near to his door. He had earlier dispatched Henry Bustle to find out the present whereabouts of former Detective Inspector Albert Greening.

The unravelling of a motive for the double murders was his highest priority, and at the forefront of his mind was the painting of HMS Duke of Wellington by Sir Thomas Craven. The note found inside the back of the artwork would only be significant if such a missive formed part of a string of other clues which had a bearing on the case. And yet, he had a strange suspicion that particular one would.

Rayner was being slowly persuaded that somewhere resting in the centre of the mystery, was a naval connection. A painting of a well-known seventy-four gun Ship of the Line, together with a brass naval button, could of course be a coincidence. On the other hand, both items could be fundamental towards piecing together the history of the two elderly victims.

There was no doubt, the killer had known the two ladies; how else would he have gained access into their property. There had been no sign of any forced entry, and according to the neighbour she had overheard a man's voice coming from inside the shop, on that same evening before Lillian Braithwaite had also heard a female's voice calling for help in the early hours of the following morning. The Detective Inspector was convinced that would have been the time when the murders had been committed, which also meant that the male visitor, if he had been the killer, had spent some hours in the sisters' company beforehand. The man had to be a relative or close friend of his victims, but what Richard Rayner needed to know, was whether the brass button bearing the insignia of HMS Victoria, had been accidentally dropped on the kitchen floor. Had it in fact been torn from a naval tunic during a struggle that would have inevitably taken place.

The Inspector continued to analyse the information he had thus far, including the marks found around Emily Barratt's neck; signs that an attempt had been made to strangle the lady, and yet there had been no mention in the Pathologist's report of similar injuries being detected on her sister, Gertrude. Also, Rayner deduced that strangulation didn't sit comfortably with being bludgeoned to death. Both ladies were frail, which meant it would not have taken much effort to strangle the life out of one, or both of them. In the detective's opinion, both attacks were separate entities. The gripping of Emily's throat having resulted during some kind of altercation, and the final death blows being administered sometime later.

The course of events that had occurred all those years before were becoming clearer in Richard Rayner's analytical mind, by the time Henry Bustle returned. The Sergeant had learned of Albert Greening's present location.

"He retired from the force some ten years ago, Inspector, and according to one of his former colleagues who still visits him on occasions, he's now living on a river boat that's permanently moored on the Thames near to St Paul's Pier."

"There's no Mrs. Greening then?"

"Oh yes, according to Sergeant Welling, the officer who keeps in touch with Greening, he has a wife still living with him, and two grown up children who both left the family nest a few years ago."

Rayner then shared his most recent thoughts with Henry Bustle, holding the Sergeant's full attention.

"According to what we have read, that button belonged to someone who was serving, or had served on HMS Victoria," the Sergeant suggested.

"I agree, or at least it's a strong possibility."

"Is it possible therefore, that the same man sent that painting of the Duke of Wellington to his mother, because he was serving on that ship at the time?"

"That is also a distinct possibility," Rayner concurred, "But although the nautical connection could be completely insignificant, I am inclined to explore that feature further. Let's go and see what Albert Greening has to offer us."

"Remembering the man myself sir, I think we shall be lucky if he offers us a cup of tea."

As the two men left Scotland Yard through the rear door, they bumped into Jack Robinson, who was just about to seek them out and give them the information he had acquired at Smithfield Market.

"Jack, you look out of breath," Rayner remarked, as the young constable bent over with both hands on his knees to assist his breathing.

"I've run all the way back, sir," he gasped, "But it was worth it."

"Catch your breath first my lad, and then share with us your good news."

Robinson straightened, and in an excited voice reported his findings.

"I managed to speak with Mr. Stanley Walker who owns the offal business at Smithfield Market. He remembered the two murdered sisters and told me they were good customers, but most of the deliveries made to their premises in Mount Street were undertaken by his son," Robinson paused to look at his notebook, before continuing, "His son's name is, Charlie Walker."

"Did his son make that last delivery on the day the double murder was committed?" Henry Bustle asked.

Robinson nodded. "Yes, according to his father, Charlie delivered early on that morning but there was something else, Stanley Walker told me. His son left home shortly after the murders, to join the Navy."

Richard Rayner's eyes widened and he glimpsed across at his Sergeant.

"I remember you both mentioned a button being found in the kitchen at Mount Street with the insignia of HMS Victoria on it," the young constable admitted, "Well, that's the ship Charlie Walker is serving on at present."

"And his father confirmed that to you?"

"Yes sir. Apparently, the ship is currently in Portsmouth as part of the reserve fleet."

"The only problem we have with that, is at the time that button was dropped at the scene of the murders, Charlie Walker would not have been wearing a naval tunic, because he was still working for his father," Rayner suggested.

Sergeant Bustle also added a comment.

"Another problem we have, is that I suspect the tunic from which that button originated, would have been worn by a naval officer."

"Yes, I agree Henry," the Inspector confirmed, "But again, it does seem co-incidental. However," he continued, turning back to Jack Robinson, "You have done well, Jack. Now go and get yourself a hot drink and we will see you back here a little later."

The young man smiled in appreciation of the compliment and quickly made his way inside the Headquarters building.

As the two detectives waited for a cab, Bustle turned and commented to his Inspector, that it did appear there was some kind of naval connection with the sisters.

"I don't think we can ignore that," he suggested.

"We are not going to Henry, but everything seems to revolve around the discovery of that brass button. We have to be wary that it might be a false trail. However, I am hoping that Albert Greening can throw some light on where the same item is now."

When the two investigators reached St Paul's Pier on the River Thames, they found to their astonishment a whole collection of narrow boats moored on the embankment leading from the pier itself to nearby New Blackfriars Bridge. The majority of the vessels were old, recently renovated narrow boats, some of which had men and women, either cleaning the exteriors or completing various decorative emblems on the sides of their individual properties.

As they slowly walked along the embankment, Bustle approached a young man who was fitting a new wooden rail to the stern of one of the barges. When asked if he was aware of a man by the name of Albert Greening, he shook his head before disappearing inside the cabin. Another older man, wearing a cloth cap, appeared and suggested the detectives looked for a boat bearing the name of, 'Charlotte' on the side.

"Look further up the river, near to the bridge," the man indicated, "You might find the man you are looking for up there."

Rayner thanked him by tipping his brown felt top hat, before he and his Sergeant continued walking along the embankment towards Blackfriars. It didn't take them long to come across the 'Charlotte', moored close to the towpath. The hull was green in colour with the rest of the exterior covered in attractive splashes of red and cream symbols.

Standing at the side of the vessel, near to the bow and holding a piece of oily rag in one hand, was the indistinguishable figure of the retired Detective Inspector. Albert Greening was a stout man with thin greying hair and thick mutton chop whiskers, which partially covered a number of facial corrugations. He was wearing a soiled grey shirt beneath a black leather waistcoat, as if challenging the freezing conditions in which all three were standing.

Richard Rayner introduced himself and his Sergeant to the narrow boat owner, who responded by holding up his grease covered palms, challenging the wisdom of shaking hands with his visitors.

"It's good to see you again, Henry," he said, "This must be important, come into the warmth gents and I'll get Charlotte to put the kettle on."

Greening led the way down some steps into the long-enclosed cabin in which the two detectives were introduced to the lady whose name had been given to the narrow boat. She was a cheerful looking, rounded lady with grey matted hair, wearing a heavy grey sweater and a pair of woolen socks that covered her knees. There was little doubt that in her younger years, she would have been attractive, but time and hard labour had removed most of her feminine allure.

The inside of the cabin was heated by a small coal burner, and the owner invited his guests to take a seat, speaking in a voice that sounded like parched rustling leaves.

"This is quite a home, Albert," Rayner commented.

"I'm fulfilling a lifetime's ambition," the man replied, "She was a horse boat, just under seventy feet long and I could find no greater seductive simplicity of a way of life, after my retirement."

The Inspector was impressed and recognised the look of satisfaction in Greening's eyes, which was not a common feature with retired police officers. In most cases known to Rayner, men retired usually bemoaning a lack of funds, and nothing more than scant reward for working all kinds of different and lengthy hours on the streets. Years of being subjected to all kinds of abuse and, on occasions, violence from the public they served. He guessed that the boatman had been one of the original 'boiled lobsters', as beat men were often referred to by the local communities; one of the pioneers of policing in the capital, when trust and respect were hard to come by.

The proud man then continued to describe the dimensions of his home on water, with Rayner showing more than a hint of interest in the measurements and weights involved when the craft was first built. Then, as Charlotte Greening attended her husband and his visitors with mugs of hot freshly made steaming tea, the reason for the visit was made clear.

"I understand you led the Inquiry into the murders of the two sisters, Emily and, Gertrude Barratt at their Tripe Shop in Mount Street, some fifteen years ago," Rayner said.

"Ah, yes. An horrendous and brutal business. Have you caught the bastard that did that to those two harmless and fragile women?"

"No, but we have re-opened the case and I was wondering what you could tell us regarding the initial enquiries that were made?"

A plate of homemade biscuits appeared on the small table at which they were sitting, and Mrs. Greening encouraged Henry Bustle to tuck in, which he did with relish.

"I suspected at the time, that some vagrant had attacked the ladies, and still believe that remains a possibility," the former Inspector declared.

"What made you think that?"

"From some of the enquiries we made. A number of people had seen a tramp hovering around the front of the shop during the afternoon before the murders were committed."

"I found no reference to that in the reports that were filed," Rayner admitted inquisitively, "Was there any description recorded of this individual?"

"Let me see now," Greening answered, rubbing his double chin, "I recall he was a tall, straggly man, unkempt and dirty, with shoulder length hair and yes, he was wearing an old ragged overcoat." The description fitted just about every vagrant in London.

"Can you remember Albert, who those people were, who saw this tramp?"

"No, but I do recall the information came from my lads who were tasked with interviewing the local residents living in Mount Street and Turner Street though." He then went on to describe what details he could remember relating to the initial enquiries that were made, most of which Rayner had extracted from the original file.

"Can you remember any snippets of information that might have come from the local prostitutes working the area?"

Greening shook his head in silence, looking a little bemused, which confirmed to Rayner, that no such enquiries had been made.

Finally, reference was made to the brass button found on the floor of the kitchen, and the Detective Inspector asked what Greening's views were concerning that discovery.

He sat back and held an arm up before resting the back of his head on it, appearing to be indifferent.

"To be honest, I didn't give it much priority. I assumed it could have come from anywhere. There was no information telling us that a seaman had called at the house. As I've already said, the vagrant was the chief suspect throughout the investigation."

"Can you recollect what happened to that button, Albert?"

The boat man shook his head, looking a little confused, but then his wife entered into the conversation.

"It's around here somewhere, Inspector," she said, before beginning to search through various drawers of a Welsh dresser which stood at the far end of the boats interior.

"You kept it yourself?" Rayner asked accusingly.

"I forgot. Well, I was happy it had no bearing on the case and forgot all about it, until it turned up in one of my jacket pockets sometime later. I didn't want to throw it away, as I thought it might bring bad luck."

"Can you recollect whether there were any threads of material attached to it, which would be the case if the button had been forcibly snatched from a tunic?"

"Here it is," Charlotte Greening announced, handing the item to Richard Rayner, "I knew we had it somewhere."

"There's your answer Inspector," Greening suggested.

Rayner looked closely at the button, scrutinising the words 'HMS Victoria' and the miniature engraving of a ship on the front of the item. When he turned it over, there were a number of threads of cotton wrapped around the loop attached to the back. The button had not just dropped on the floor, it had been violently torn from a tunic jacket, in all

Probability. during a struggle that must have taken place before the murders were committed, as he had earlier surmised.

Henry Bustle had managed to finish off all the biscuits provided by Mrs. Greening, so his Inspector stood to leave, but before doing so, had a few more questions to put to the former officer in charge of the case.

"Tell me Albert, did you attend the funerals?"

Greening also stood from his chair and replied, "I most certainly did, out of respect."

"Did you notice any strangers at the service standing amongst the mourners, or possibly watching from a distance?"

"That would have been impossible, as the whole district seemed to be in attendance. There were hundreds there, and I had to post a couple of constables around the graveside to maintain some dignity for the victims."

"I understand. One last question; did you know whether either of the sisters had been married?"

"Not as far as I was aware."

"Thank you. And thank you Mrs. Greening for your kind hospitality. We might have to call again, if that's alright? But I shall do my very best to leave you to your peaceful retirement."

"Of course Inspector. You will always be made welcome here and that goes for your Sergeant, who undoubtedly enjoys my biscuits."

Henry Bustle nodded his appreciation, but could not avoid belching at the same time, having left the plate of biscuits empty.

Chapter Four

"What in God's name are you doing here Constable Robinson?"

Young Jack had the misfortune of bumping into Superintendent Morgan in the corridor outside Richard Rayner's office, whilst chatting to a colleague and friend who was also assisting the Detective Department in another section of Scotland Yard.

"I'm waiting for Inspector Rayner sir," he answered, looking both embarrassed and nervous.

"Then you'll bloody be waiting a long time lad," Morgan bawled back at him, "One thing you will soon learn from working with Rayner, is that he tends to disappear from time to time, and re-appears when it suits him."

"Yes sir."

"Should you cross his path sometime today, then tell him I want to see him, if of course he can spare me the time."

"Yes sir. I mean I will sir."

The young constable stood dumbfounded, as he watched Frederick Morgan strutting away, heading for his own office.

When the two detectives finally appeared, the young constable passed on the message to the Inspector and Rayner immediately made his way to his senior officer's room.

The Superintendent was in his usual place, sitting behind his desk, just about to light up a pipe full of tobacco and fill his office with more pungent smoke.

"So, you've decided to make an appearance," the senior man declared, his passion for sarcasm almost amounting to an obsession.

"We have been extremely busy sir, but I believe we are making some head way."

"Let me be the judge of that, Rayner. Please do continue."

The Detective Inspector then related to Morgan details of what they had learned from their visit to the scene of the murders, including the possible nautical connection involving the painting and brass button recovered from Albert Greening. He also spoke of what Jack Robinson had discovered concerning Charlie Walker's decision to join the Navy, and the fact he was posted to HMS Victoria.

When he had finished his briefing, Frederick Morgan sat back in his chair and quietly asked, "What was your opinion of Albert Greening and the way he handled the case initially?"

"To be honest with you sir, I was not impressed and believe the enquiries made at the time did not probe sufficiently." Rayner made mention of the mysterious vagrant referred to by Greening, with very few follow-up enquiries having been made.

As the outline of Morgan's figure began to fade behind the inevitable clouds of blue smoke, the Superintendent continued to express his personal opinion of the initial investigation.

"Albert Greening was an honest man, but unfortunately he was the kind of Inspector who liked to cut corners, and from what you have told me that appears to have been apparent in this particular case. Why in God's name did he retain possession of the tunic button?"

"The reason he gave, when asked, was that he thought it irrelevant."

Rayner could just about make out the anger in Morgan's eyes, and waited for more severe criticism to be thrown in the direction of the retired Inspector, but it never materialised. Instead, the Superintendent suddenly blurted out, "Charlie Walker's your man, Inspector. There are too many co-incidences in my book for him not to have been involved."

"I have my doubts sir. We need to complete more groundwork on the suggestion that there was a vagrant in the area at the time, but I shall keep Walker in mind, obviously."

"Let's bring him in and see how he behaves under interrogation." It was more of a command than a suggestion, and the Superintendent stood from his chair after placing his smoking pipe on top of his desk, and scratching at his testicles.

"I shall be catching an overnight train from Waterloo to Portsmouth later to interview the man, if he is still posted to the Victoria, and is available."

Morgan was tempted to make a further derogatory remark about the immaculate attire of his Inspector, but then thought better of it and just signaled that the interview had ended by a wave of his hand.

After leaving the Superintendent's office, Rayner made his way back to his own where he found both Henry Bustle and Jack Robinson waiting. If he was to catch the overnight train to Portsmouth that same evening, time was running short, so he quickly tasked the two other men with what he required them to do in his absence.

"We need to find out more regarding the victims Henry," he suggested to his Sergeant, "Each of the sister's background and whether they were both truly spinsters, or had been married in the long distant past."

"I'll get on to that straight away."

"I want you Jack, to trace the, Braithwaites who lived next door to the Tripe Shop at the time of the murders. In particular, Lillian Braithwaite and find out if they had any knowledge of a vagrant being in the locality during the day prior to the crimes being committed. If you have any difficulty with that, Sergeant Bustle will assist you."

"Yes sir, I will pay a visit to Mount Street immediately."

"Thank you. Now I'm off gentlemen to Portsmouth and hope to be back sometime late tomorrow. We can meet back here tomorrow evening and exchange any useful information we have come across."

"How much credence are you giving to the vagrant mentioned by Albert Greening, Inspector?" Henry Bustle asked.

"I think at this time Sergeant, we have to treat every possibility seriously, at the same time remaining open minded."

Richard Rayner had been concerned that the snow might have brought the train network to a halt, and was relieved to discover from the Station Master at Waterloo that the one he was due to catch, was on time and the majority of the lines had been cleared.

"Mind you sir," the man with a large grey bushy moustache explained, "There's no guarantee you will be travelling back from Portsmouth tomorrow. If this snow gets much worse, there might be further problems."

"Thank you," Rayner said, before heading for his train.

On the journey to the south coast, the Detective Inspector concentrated his mind on the young man he was going to visit. Although he remained doubtful that Charlie Walker was indeed the killer they were hunting, only because at the time the HMS Victoria button was recovered from the scene, the suspect had not yet joined up. Also, as Henry Bustle had mentioned previously, the kind of tunic button Rayner now had in his possession, would almost certainly have come from a naval officer's uniform.

When his train eventually pulled into Portsmouth Harbour Railway Station, following a few hours sleep the detective had managed to take advantage of, the man from Scotland Yard was impressed by what he found to be a newly built terminal. The building stood on a wooden pier at the side of Portsmouth's Gunwharf Quays in the harbour. As soon as he left the station, he was amazed at the amount of building work that appeared to be ongoing. There were numerous houses springing up all over the town, which signaled a vast increase in the local population. Undoubtedly, Portsmouth was in the grip of some kind of accelerated expansion.

The first seaman he came across was a mariner wearing three broad stripes on one arm and Rayner enquired as to whether the man knew the whereabouts of HMS Victoria.

"Aye," the man said in a gruff voice, "She's berthed with the rest of the reserve fleet down in the harbour, near to where the Victory is in dry dock." Of course, he was referring to Vice Admiral Nelson's flagship at the Battle of Trafalgar.

The visitor tipped his hat, before heading towards the collection of sailing masts which indicated the harbour. The town was busy with seamen, naval officers, labourers, brickies and horse drawn cabbies, intermingling with each other like swarms of ants all heading towards their individual nests. When he finally reached his destination, Rayner took a moment to admire HMS Victory, which was covered with men working on rope ladders, with tins of paint and brushes in their hands.

This was where the most famous sailor in Britain's naval history had made his well-known speech to the crew of the Victory and dockyard workers, before leaving Portsmouth to command the fleet, some seventy years before. 'England expects every man will do his duty'.

It was a message that sent shivers down the Inspector's spine, and he stood glued to the spot, watching the current day seamen at work. He couldn't help but feel in awe of Nelson's Flag Ship and the history that was attached to it. Finally, when he came out of his reverie, he noticed a young naval officer standing on the quayside, watching over a number of men who were assisting with the refitting of the Victory.

In response to introducing himself to the officer, he was saluted and informed, "Lieutenant Grimshaw at your service, sir. How can I be of help to you?"

"I'm looking for the location of HMS Victoria, lieutenant."

"Right sir, the Victoria is currently in the Rigging Basin for repairs. That's next to the Tidal Basin, just north of the Royal Dockyard."

"Actually, I need to speak with one of the crew on Victoria. Will there be any officer on board that I could make such arrangements with?"

"In that case, I recommend you speak with the Master at Arms. His office is in Admiralty House and I am sure he will be able to assist you." The naval officer then gave Rayner directions, emphasising that the Headquarters building wasn't far away from where they were standing.

Again, the Inspector from Scotland Yard appreciated the assistance given to him and thanked the lieutenant, before turning to walk away from the quay, heading towards the town. Having left the harbour, he turned left and soon recognised the building he sought. It was a large white domain which stood in an elevated position on top of a hill, requiring a great deal of effort to reach as Richard Rayner was to soon find out, preparing himself for a challenging climb.

The Master-at-Arms was a position first introduced to the Royal Navy in the seventeenth century, and was responsible for a ship's small arms and other weapons, in addition to teaching the crews how to use them. He was also tasked with the overall discipline of the men, and the man Rayner soon found himself facing was in total contrast to the image he had been anticipating. Instead of a colossus gripping a Cat O Nine Tails in one hand, and a flagon of rum in the other, he was surprised to see a slim man, of average height, with a shaven head and drooping moustache, the ends of which touched his chin.

Elias Gardiner spoke with a Bristol accent when he introduced himself, before asking the detective from London how he could assist.

Rayner explained the reason for his visit to Portsmouth, before, Gardiner asked him to wait. He then left the office and was away for a few minutes, allowing time for the detective to view a number of framed prints of various ships, carefully placed on each of the walls.

When he returned, the Master-at-Arms explained that he had sent a rating down to the Victoria to try and find the location of Charlie Walker.

"Might I ask the reason why you wish to see Seaman Walker, Inspector?"

"I am investigating a serious incident that took place in London some fifteen years ago, and believe that Seaman Walker might be able to assist," Rayner explained.

"As a witness or a suspect?"

"Both."

"I see. Well I'm sure you are aware that any action taken against a naval rating must be conducted through the Admiralty."

The Inspector nodded his understanding, and then produced the brass button from his pocket, before showing it to Gardiner.

"In all your experience of being a mariner, what can you tell me about that, sir."

The man looked at it closely, before confirming, "It's a button that has come from an officer's jacket, who at the time of wearing it was posted to HMS Victoria, or so it might seem."

"Any idea what rank the owner would have held?"

"Not really, except he wasn't a captain or above, as they have a different insignia on the button to their tunics. There are occasions when a ship such as the Victoria is deployed as a training vessel, and during that period individual officers who join the ship for that purpose, could obtain uniforms which bear the ship's credentials. That doesn't necessarily mean they would hold an active position on the officers list."

"So, for example, a lieutenant who normally works on one war ship could be temporarily transferred to another, which is being used as a training ship. The same officer, before completing his secondment, would have access to uniforms designated to the permanent officers of that same training ship?"

"Exactly, and what I am saying is that, although that particular button bears the name of HMS Victoria, that doesn't confirm that the wearer was a permanent member of that ship's list of officers."

The news wasn't warmly welcomed by Richard Rayner, having to now acknowledge that the owner of the button found at the scene of the murders, could have been any serving officer in the Royal Navy, below the rank of captain.

There was a knock on the door and the Master called for the individual to enter.

A young seaman stepped into the office and explained that he had found Seaman Walker and the rating was standing outside.

Chapter Five

Charlie Walker was a short stocky man with fair hair, dressed in a white collarless shirt beneath a blue boiler suit. His pale face bore witness to any assertion that the seaman had not spent that many of the past few years at sea. His dark brown eyes stared across at the Detective Inspector, as he clicked his heels together and saluted the Master in navy fashion.

Gardiner introduced, Inspector Rayner, before asking if the detective had any objections to him remaining during the interview that was to take place.

Rayner agreed to the request, and Seaman Walker was invited to take a chair, next to the dandy from London.

The Inspector wasted little time in asking questions that were direct and meaningful.

"Before joining the navy Charlie, I understand you worked for your father as a deliveryman, is that correct?"

"Aye aye sir. I mean Yes sir," the sailor answered confidently. He seemed to be a bright fellow, who was self-assured, which would have been a product of years of naval discipline.

"Do you remember delivering offal to the elderly sisters who had a Tripe Shop in Mount Street, on the corner of Turner Street?"

"Yes sir. It was a regular delivery."

"How well did you get to know those two women Charlie?"

"Quite well sir. They usually gave me some tea and occasionally a bowl of Tripe and Onions. Is this about their murders sir?"

"Yes it is. Do you know anything about that incident?"

"No sir," the man answered, shaking his head and showing no signs of guilt in his eyes.

"I understand you delivered to them on the day before they were murdered. Can you remember doing that?"

"Yes sir. Two boxes wrapped in muslin."

"You have quite a good memory Charlie, seeing as it was fifteen years ago."

"It was always two boxes wrapped in muslin sir. Their delivery never changed."

"But can you remember going there on that particular day?"

"Yes, because the following day we heard about the murders, and I mentioned to those I worked with about having made a delivery there, on the day before.

Charlie Walker's answers and his confident manner added more doubt to any suspicion Richard Rayner might have held as to his guilt.

"I want you to try and cast your mind back to that particular day, which would have been the last time you delivered to the sisters' shop. Was there anything about them that appeared to be unusual? The way they spoke to you, or acted?"

The naval rating again shook his head, and gave the question some thought, before answering, "They were the same as normal sir. I remember Miss Emily took the boxes from me, and Miss Gertrude mentioned something about having had a sleepless night because of all the racket going on across at the hospital."

"Did she say what kind of racket?"

"No sir. I assumed she was referring to ambulances going in and out on a busy night."

"Again, think carefully about the time you were there. Did they mention anything about a vagrant acting suspiciously, or did you see one loitering around outside the shop?"

After giving more consideration to the question, Charlie answered with certainty, "No sir."

"Once you had made that delivery, did you ever have cause to return to the shop later that same day?"

"No sir. There was no call to."

"Why did you decide to join the navy at that particular time, Charlie?"

"I didn't sir. I had been thinking about joining up for some time before that, and after my father got a replacement delivery man, thought that was the best time to do so."

"Very well Charlie, you have been most helpful," Rayner said, "By the way, have you ever served on the Duke of Wellington?"

"No sir."

"Thank you for giving me your time. What kind of work are you engaged in at the moment?"

The man smiled broadly and explained, "Nothing very exciting sir, just greasing the anchor in the bow."

Rayner smiled back, but then the Master piped up with a few enquiries of his own.

"Before you get back to work seaman, tell us this. Were you ever interviewed by a naval officer prior to your application being accepted?"

"No sir."

"Did you ever come across a naval officer at those premises the Inspector has been talking about?"

Charlie seemed to hesitate, and brushed some invisible fluff off his trouser legs, obviously giving some thought to what the Master had asked. He then looked directly at Rayner, as if just having made an important decision, and explained in a quiet, almost solemn voice.

"Now I come to think of it, when Miss Emily took the boxes of tripe from me, I followed her to the far corner of the shop where she laid the first box down. She then took the second box off me, and carried it out through the back. I think she was going to store it in the kitchen."

"You are certain about that, Charlie?"

"Yes sir, but I followed her into the corridor that runs between the shop and the back room, and noticed someone sitting on a sofa inside the private quarters there. I didn't see much of him, but it was definitely a man because he was wearing bell bottom trousers."

"A seaman?" the Master asked.

"I think so, and probably an officer sir, because he was wearing brightly polished shoes, but I seem to remember he wasn't wearing a jacket, just a white shirt. I didn't pay much attention to him, because I was thinking more of Miss Emily who was carrying the second box of tripe."

"Were any words spoken at that time Charlie?" Rayner asked, recovering the interview.

"No sir, not that I'm aware of, but it was the sight of those bell bottoms that got me to thinking it was time to apply for the mob."

The room went quiet momentarily, whilst the Inspector gave more thought to what had just been disclosed. Then he turned once again to the seaman and asked, "Is there anything else about that man you can tell me about, such as was he smoking? Did you smell tobacco smoke or anything else in the air? Did he move from the sofa at any time?"

"No sir, as I said, I didn't pay much attention to him."

"Did you wonder why the man was there, sitting in the back room?"

"No sir, once I left, I didn't give him any further thought, until now that is."

"And you didn't see his face or anything that might describe him?"

"Sorry, no sir."

Richard Rayner thanked the seaman once again, and suggested that if Charlie Walker remembered anything else about that final visit to the sisters' shop, he was to contact him at Scotland Yard. He handed the man one of his calling cards, before the young man stood and left, after once again saluting the Master-at-Arms.

"I hope you found your visit fruitful Inspector," Gardiner remarked.

"I most certainly have sir," he replied, "And thank you for your assistance."

An exhausted Detective Inspector stayed that night in a hotel near to the harbour, and was appreciative the following morning that no more heavy snow had fallen, leaving the tracks clear and the trains running. On his way back to the capital he made some notes of everything Charlie Walker had mentioned to him regarding the naval visitor to the victims' home on that fateful day. Yet another piece to the jigsaw had been unearthed, and for the first time Richard Rayner was beginning to feel optimistic about finding the killer. Now he was convinced of that naval connection he had previously suspected.

As he had predicted, it was late by the time his return train pulled into Waterloo, and he caught a cab to Scotland Yard where he found Henry Bustle waiting in his office.

The first question he asked his Sergeant was for the whereabouts of young Jack Robinson?"

"I haven't seen the lad since we left the office this morning. He told me he'd discovered that the Braithwaites had left that house next to the sisters' shop a couple of years after the murders, and was having some difficulty in tracing where they had gone to. I advised him to make a few enquiries at the local church, just in case the clergy remembered them."

Rayner took his seat behind his desk and pondered further on the visit he'd just undertaken.

"Did you have much joy Inspector, in Portsmouth?" the Sergeant asked.

Rayner briefly explained what had been learnt from Charlie Walker; particularly regarding the appearance of what the seaman believed was a naval officer, sitting in the victims' back parlour on the day before the murders.

Henry Bustle stood from the chair he'd been occupying, obviously excited about what his Inspector had just shared with him.

"And the lad believed the visitor was a naval officer," he spoke out, reiterating what Rayner had already announced, "Then we have him. That button must have come from him during some violent quarrel he had with the sisters."

"Not so fast Henry," the Inspector said in a calming voice, "We still have to identify him, and I suspect that will only come from somewhere in the victims' antecedents. There is still mention of the loitering vagrant which we have to bottom out. How did you fare these last two days?"

"I think my throbbing bunion will tell you I have done a lot of leg work visiting various habitats and institutions, mostly in the Whitechapel district, but my endeavours have, I think, been rewarded."

The Sergeant then went on to explain that, both Emily and Gertrude were born and raised in Coventry by their father, Bartholomew Barratt, following their mother's premature death from Cholera. After the loss of his wife, the old man sold his lucrative business as a cabinet maker and brought his daughters' down to London, where all three lived for some years in Bermondsey, a district in which their father opened and ran a small furniture shop.

"But there's more. The interesting thing is that there is a record at the Bermondsey Parish Church of one, Gertrude Barratt, registering the birth of a son who was named, and later Christened as Herbert Barratt, some forty-five years ago."

Rayner stood from his seat and rested both hands on the desk top, leaning across towards his Sergeant, looking extremely confounded.

"Yes," Bustle continued, "It seems that the boy was a bastard, born out of wedlock as there was no record of the father."

"It also confirms that the seafaring painting we found at the Mount Street address was sent to, Gertrude Barratt, by her son, Herbert."

The Sergeant then continued to describe the way in which he had learnt that following Bartholomew Barratt's death, the two sisters then moved into Mount Street and opened their Tripe Shop.

"Although I have not been able to confirm the size of the ladies wealth, I suspect that following their father's departure, they were both left fairly well off."

"The mysterious naval officer who visited their shop on that dreadful day could very well be the same person who sent his mother that portrait of HMS Duke of Wellington," Rayner suggested.

"I think that is highly likely Inspector. Do you think he could be the man we are looking for?"

"I'm not so sure Henry. For what purpose would a man brutally murder his own mother and aunt, if that was the case?"

"Who knows what desperate act a man might commit if he falls on hard times and becomes destitute sir."

Constable Jack Robinson had also been working diligently in trying to track down Lillian and Thomas Braithwaite, having learned that the couple had moved from their Mount Street address some thirteen years earlier. After speaking with a number of people who were residents in the locality his enquiries still drew a blank. He then decided to follow Sergeant Bustle's advice and approach the local parson, The Reverend Walter Mitchell at St Mary's Church, which was situated in Adler Street on the corner with Whitechapel High Street.

The Reverend was a tall, spindly man with unruly white hair, dressed in all black from his jacket to his stockings, with a pair of black shiny buckled shoes covering his feet. At first the parson viewed his young visitor with suspicion, but when it became obvious that the constable was trying to trace the two Braithwaite's, he immediately became informative.

"Lillian Braithwaite still attends my Sunday services, but alas, her husband Thomas, a good man at heart, passed away not more than a couple of years ago," Walter Mitchell admitted, "Leaving the wretched woman to fend for herself. Fortunately, they were childless."

"Do you know Reverend, where Mrs. Braithwaite lives now?" the young constable asked, holding his pencil and notebook in both hands.

"Of course, I know where all of my parishioners live, that is when they are not defying God's Law and wasting their hard-earned pennies in the local brew houses. Now let me see, I'm not sure of the number but you will find the impoverished lady living in some hovel in Finch Street, across the way from the hospital."

"How does she appear to be to you sir? I mean as far as her health is concerned?"

"Not well; not well at all. She is plagued with a constant cough and refuses any charitable assistance. Please give her my kindest regards when you see her young man."

Jack left, pleased with how his hard work was now appearing to show some kind of reward. When he reached Finch Street, Whitechapel, it didn't take long for the officer to find the lady he sought. Having sought the help of some street urchins, he was escorted down a narrow back alley to the lady's front door. In appreciation, the constable was obliged to part with a few pennies in return for their assistance.

"Will you be wanting an escort back to your carriage mister?" one of the street tramps enquired, pushing his luck.

Robinson just smiled at the group and thanked them again for their help, before they scattered, as if someone had just called them to dinner.

The back to back small terraced house in which Lillian Braithwaite was now living, faced a square court with cobbles laden with all kinds of garbage and filth, most of which was covered in snow.

He found the front door wide open, so stood on the step, calling the lady's name.

Lillian was now grey headed with lines engraved across her face that confirmed the hardship she had experienced in recent years. Her cheeks were hollow and her eyes displayed the same disenchantment and desperation, common to those who lived in poverty and squalor. Although the woman was obviously at her wits end, she still offered to make tea for her young visitor, who declined, feeling embarrassed that she could ill afford to spare even a spoonful of tea leaves.

She remembered the night of the double murders well, and did not have to be reminded of the role she had played.

The constable wrote down virtually every word Lillian recited to him, asking the most pertinent questions to which she answered truthfully. When he made mention of the vagrant allegedly seen loitering near to the victims' shop close to the time the murders were committed, her response was surprising. Lillian Braithwaite instantly admitted having not only seen the tramp, but elaborating further with the fact that he was known to her, and had often been a visitor to the locality around the time of the sisters' demise.

Once satisfied he had exhausted all the information from the witness, the constable bade her farewell, but not before surreptitiously leaving a few coins on a small table near the door. As he began his journey back to Scotland Yard, young Jack Robinson was completely oblivious to the figure in the shadows that was still watching over him, in similar fashion to a hunter stalking his prey, and waiting for the right time to pounce.

Chapter Six

Frederick Morgan's facial features were puce with rage. The Superintendent had gone beyond being incensed, and his hostility was compounded more with each page of the newspaper he read. Accusations of incompetency and lethargy flew out from the printed articles with the force of projectiles possessing a stinging effect. The press was even blaming Richard Rayner for being dilatory in his efforts to find the killer of the two Barratt sisters.

"Have you read this garbage," the senior detective roared, as his Inspector walked through the door, "The bastards have compiled damning fiction from a barrage of misquotes. I shall commence libel actions against every one of them."

Rayner was dressed in his usual impeccable brown frock coat with a velvet collar and matching cravat, as he sat in a leather chair and smiled back at the Superintendent, in his usual tenacious manner.

"I fear the newspapers have always been the same, but at least they are quick to acknowledge our successes when they are achieved. In my opinion, the most effective way we can denounce such literary nonsense is to bring the killer to justice."

"And have you come to tell me of your success in finally identifying the killer, or better still, charging somebody?"

"We have made considerable progress, and I do believe there is some light at the end of the tunnel Superintendent."

"Whose bloody tunnel are you referring to Rayner?"

The Detective Inspector then continued to explain what he and Sergeant Bustle had unraveled thus far, not forgetting to mention Constable Jack Robinson.

"The young man has worked hard, and managed to track down the woman, Lillian Braithwaite, yesterday. I think he might have identified the vagrant I mentioned previously, who was seen loitering around the Tripe Shop before the murders were committed."

"God only knows I'm in dire need of some positive news to tell the Commissioner."

"It seems that, according to Lillian Braithwaite, there used to be a homeless tramp known to the locals as Peter Tinman."

Morgan shuffled in his seat, as if anticipating a sudden attack of Shingles.

"Pray tell me, what kind of name is that?"

"It's not his actual name," Rayner confirmed, "Apparently he was known as 'The Tinman', or 'Peter the Tinman', only for the fact the man collected pieces of disregarded tin off the streets and sold them for a paltry sum to whatever metal merchant he did business with. Anyway, again, according to the lady, Peter Tinman would hang around the locality looking for scraps of food, or begging the same from various people, and our two sisters were apparently a favourite visiting place for the vagrant."

"It seems that just about everybody regarded them as Angels of Mercy," Morgan quipped, with a hint of sarcasm contained in the crackle of his authoritative voice.

"Well, he was encouraged to visit them fairly frequently as a result of hot bowls of tripe they would feed him with."

"So where is this Tinman now?"

"The man's present location eludes us, but at least we have a name to identify him by and in fairness, after fifteen years, he could be anywhere in the country. Henry Bustle is out as we speak, making some enquiries."

The Irish Rookery, otherwise known to locals as, 'The Holy Land', was one of the poorest districts in London. It was also a favourite haunt of criminals, vagabonds and itinerants. Located in St Giles in the Field, the area comprised of a network of narrow cobbled alleyways, squares and courts, frequented by hordes of pick-pockets, prostitutes and other undesirables. The multitude of hovels had mostly dirt floors and fronted unpaved streets devoid of gas lighting or drainage. Open sewers encouraged disease amongst the population, which resulted in many of the inhabitants displaying sunken eyes and pot marked skin. The Holy Land was indeed, an alien territory compared to the rest of London.

Visitors to the theatre of vice and poverty, had to initially overcome the stench that came from both properties and streets alike. Those paying customers with sufficient courage to enter the district seeking their pleasure in the numerous brothels, usually left having replaced their thirst for lust with a dose of the pox.

Many of the residents were Irish migrants who had fled from their own country to escape the potato famine, only to find that the grass on the other side wasn't as green as they might have hoped. They had become a law unto themselves, and the occasional homicide resulting from some violent argument or altercation, in most cases, were dealt with by their own people. The police were rarely invited to make their own enquiries. Those who dared to venture into the sin bin were usually met by open hostility and the occasional bout of violence.

Henry Bustle knew the slum district well, having spent most of his younger years as a patrolling constable, either investigating crime or cultivating one or two informants who were useful to him. As he made his way down one particular alleyway, towards the Elephant and Jackal, a public house situated nearby, he found the obnoxious stink hadn't abated since his last visit. It was a case of hanging around, until his nostrils finally shook hands with the fetid smell of decay and human excrement.

The individual the Sergeant was attempting to seek out was sitting in a far corner of the dark and grim looking bar room. A group of other men, all speaking vociferously with Irish accents, were standing at the bar, exchanging meaningless conversation with a barman. The same attendant broke away to serve, Henry Bustle to a glass of brackish tasting ale.

"Haven't seen you in here for some time Sergeant," the barman said, as he handed over the drink, speaking sufficiently loud enough for the other men to take note that a detective was in their presence.

As far as Bustle was concerned, it was all part of the game he played, and winked an eye at the barman, in acknowledgement of the man's cunning. It was also a threatening gesture to confirm that if anything kicked off, the human warning system would be the first in the line of fire. He then carried his drink across the room, to sit next to the lone individual in the corner.

The Sergeant's informant was an elderly man, who had obviously seen better times. Wearing well-worn rags with a filthy red woolen hat on a head covered in grey hair, the man with the thin, jaundiced face raised his glass of porter to the visitor.

"How are things with you Howie?" the visitor from Scotland Yard asked quietly.

"Not good Mr. Bustle. Not good at all," Howie croaked, before being subjected to a prolonged coughing fit, which took a minute or two to subside, "It's the consumption you see, get's worse by the day."

"Have you seen a doctor about it?" Bustle enquired, genuinely.

"And who would pay for that privilege?" His man then paused, before lowering his voice further, and advising, "You shouldn't be here, you know that."

"I need some help. I'm trying to put my hands on an old vagrant known as Peter the Tinman. Any ideas, Howie?"

The old man looked surprised at first, before asking, "What do you want with him? He's a harmless old man who keeps himself to himself."

"Not so harmless from what I've been told. I only want to talk to him, so where is he my old friend?"

"He ain't been around here for a long time," Howie confirmed, "But you might try looking up the Whitechapel Road; that's the last place I heard he was hanging around, Mr. Bustle."

"You can do better than that, Howie," the Sergeant suggested, taking a florin from his jacket pocket and placing it on top of the drinks table.

The coin disappeared as quickly as the old man produced a closed hand from beneath the table, as speedily as a snake's tongue hitting its prey. Then he began to suggest he would make some enquiries to pin point The Tinman's exact location, but before he could finish the two men had company. Four of the group of hard men, who had been standing conversing with the barman, moved closer to Bustle and his man.

"You can smell it from here," one well-built, muscular Irishman loudly declared to one of the other louts.

"That's funny Bernard. All I can sniff is boiled lobster," the other answered insincerely, again in a broad Dublin accent.

Henry Bustle had been here before, and knew that the only way he was going to leave that room was by fighting his way out. So, not wanting to waste time, he stood from his chair with clenched fists and his scar reddening down the side of his face. He menacingly responded to the jibes by explaining, "The only smell in here gents, is that of Irish peat farmers, and the shit in which they wallow."

That was the trigger point for kicking off the violence that would inevitably follow. Either the Detective Sergeant would walk out of that drinking hovel with a few cuts and bruises, or he would be thrown out head first, unconscious and requiring the services of a hospital physician.

Bernard was the first to react by kicking the table to one side, which separated himself from their opponent, before throwing the first punch, intending to knock Bustle's head from his shoulders. But the Sergeant was ready and managed to duck the first intended strike, responding by kicking the big Irishman in the groin. That was Bernard temporarily disabled, but there were three more obstacles willing to participate in the latest battle of The Elephant and Jackal.

The man from Scotland Yard managed to club two of the others down to the floorboards, before the fourth heavy ruffian dug a fist into Bustle's ribs. He then followed up by stinging the back of the Sergeant's head with a telling blow, which sent the detective reeling down to the sticky floor.

Bustle quickly turned on to his back and with all the strength in his two legs, kicked number four in the knee cap, which resulted in a painful scream. By the time the Sergeant recovered his feet, so had the first three assailants, who in military fashion spread themselves out in a straight line between their opponent and the exit door, daring their man to attempt his escape. But Henry being Henry, had never been the kind of man to lay down his arms. Any inkling of surrendering to lay-a-bouts such as these, was alien to him and with his anger now at full pitch, he leapt at all three of them, flaying them with both heavy fists, some punches landing, others missing their target. But his opponents hit back, and his head and body were pummeled by rapid fire, the bullets in reality being heavy boots and shovel-like fists.

Even Richard Rayner's right-hand man could not sustain the strength required to see off such heavy opposition. Incapable of continuing, he lay there, feeling the excruciating pain continue, until finally one of the Irish Navvies declared, "That's it Pat; he's had enough."

There were sneers and jeers, as the men finally left the public house, bragging of their latest victory. Henry Bustle felt that every one of his ribs were no longer intact. His mouth was full of blood and his ugly face masked by the same red stuff. It had been a few years since the Sergeant had been on the receiving end of such a beating, but whether it had been worth it, had still yet to be discovered.

Both his informant, Howie, and the bar man helped the semi-conscious man to his feet, and Bustle's gallant, if not stupid effort, was rewarded with a glass of half decent brandy, supplied by the proprietor and which immediately set the inside of his mouth on fire.

As they slowly walked him towards the exit door, having already escorted the victim on a few laps of the room in an attempt to bring the casualty back to the real world, Howie whispered in his ear, "Your man can be found every evening at the Jewish Soup Kitchen in Leman Street, Spitalfields."

It was a few hours later when the battered and hideous face of Detective Sergeant Henry Bustle appeared in the doorway of Inspector Rayner's office.

"Good God, Henry. What in tarnation has happened to you?" the Inspector enquired with surprise and incredulity.

Although it pained the Sergeant to even speak, he managed to blurt out the words, "We'll find The Tinman at the Jewish Soup Kitchen in Leman Street, Spittalfields... tonight."

Rayner stepped across his office to support his favoured detective, before helping him to a soft chair and suggesting he should go to hospital. But Bustle rejected the idea, preferring to be taken home to the loving care of his wife, even if it meant having to listen to four excitable kids in the background.

"Very well my friend, if you are sure." His Sergeant would not be going anywhere in the next few days, apart from his own bed where his wife would undoubtedly give him the appropriate nursing and care. Yet, Bustle's absence was going to create a problem for the Inspector, who quietly cursed to himself as he collected his coat before taking the severely injured casualty home.

Chapter Seven

A few hours had passed by since the last fall of snow, but as the darkness of night began to close in the temperature dropped dramatically, turning the London pavements and thoroughfares into sheets of frozen ice. It was extremely hazardous for both horse-drawn vehicles and pedestrians, and both Richard Rayner and Jack Robinson could not avoid slipping and falling, as they made their way through the darkness of the narrow passageways of Spitalfields. By the time they reached their objective, hips, elbows and knees had sustained heavy bruising with both men having visited the slippery cobble stones.

From a shop doorway in Leman Street, the two police officers watched the front of the Jewish Shelter, which was a charitable venture supported by the wealthier Jews, to offer some comfort to the poorer members of their community. Their pains and discomforts were soon forgotten when they viewed the line of men and women standing outside the entrance to the building. They were all, without exception, homeless individuals; poor and destitute souls whose survival in such severe winter conditions depended purely on the free nourishment on offer.

It was quite common in that part of London to find a corpse lying in some alleyway, frozen to death having died from Malnutrition or Hypothermia. Burials were frequent, and little time was spent in trying to identify the deceased, resulting in a large number of unmarked graves. For those whose Christian beliefs motivated them to help in what way they could, it was like plugging a hole in a dam, where forty others existed. Yet, for the majority who had been overwhelmed by apathy, and turned their backs on other people's problems, those selfish attitudes helped to maintain their own comfort zones.

Towards the back of the queue, standing beneath a gas lamp, was a tall, straggly individual with shoulder length grey hair. The man's corrugated and weathered face gave testimony to many years having been spent on the streets. The grizzled vagrant, like so many of the other homeless individuals, appeared to be disillusioned, which was not surprising, considering the circumstances in which they had to survive.

"It could be him Inspector," young Robinson agreed, after Rayner had pointed out the tallest man in the queue, "According to Mrs. Braithwaite's description, but she was thinking back fifteen years ago."

"He certainly looks as though he is in dire need of something hot inside him; in fact, they all do Jack so let's wait until our man has taken advantage of the charity being offered."

It didn't take long for the individual they suspected to be Peter the Tinman, to reach the entrance and disappear inside, the queue never really diminishing, as other less fortunate souls joined it. As soon as their suspect had gone inside, the two policemen, led by Rayner, stepped across the icy road, and were met by a heavily built man at the front door, wearing a flea-bitten fur coat. They were allowed access as soon as the Inspector explained who they were, and no questions were asked to the reason why they were there, not that the doorman would have been given any.

Through an open alcove, they could see into a small room at the back of the Shelter. There were wooden crates visible, upon which the unfortunates were sat, as bowls of hot soup were dished out and placed before them on long planks that represented tables. Some of the recipients used spoons that were provided, and others just drank directly from the steaming bowls, many then pleading for more, but refused. A strict rule that one bowl only was afforded to each individual had to be adhered to.

Rayner watched closely, as their suspect drank his soup slowly, as if it was the last meal he would ever relish, and using a spoon to do so. He spoke with no one and remained engrossed in the limited fare presented to him. Whatever garments the vagrant was wearing were invisible beneath a large tattered trench coat that reached his ankles, obviously having been handed down to him, or having been stolen from someone's dwelling. What was certain was that the coat had been on the same shoulders for a long time, owing to its poor condition.

The tramp was also wearing a pathetic pair of woolen mittens with the fingers worn out, which he never took off. After finally finishing his daily meal, he wiped his mouth with the back of a gloved hand, before sitting motionless, allowing the warmth of the room to envelop him.

"You would think they would provide some bread, Inspector,"

Robinson remarked.

"It's all about how much money they have to spend Jack. I'm sure if the good people who run this place could have afforded to buy bread for these impoverished people, it would be on the table."

Then, seeing the tall man stand from the table, Rayner moved quickly, entering the room and approaching the vagrant, wary that in the circumstances, the man might just turn violent. The detective's attire was certainly in vivid contrast to those who were present in the same dining room, causing a few eyebrows to be raised.

"Peter Tinman?" the Inspector quietly asked, wanting to create as little fuss as possible.

The suspect's eyes widened and his mouth opened. His whole initial demeanour was one of an individual about to respond by physically striking out. But the vagrant remained calm as Rayner just stood there, facing him and pitifully smiling.

The Detective Inspector was undoubtedly a skilled and clever linguist, but he was also a highly proficient diplomat, who believed that if any kind of violence could be avoided by words or behaviour, it would be. Richard Rayner's wide repertoire of phraseology served him well, whether debating a subject or situation with the Commissioner of the Metropolitan Police, or when requesting a street vagrant to escort him to Scotland Yard.

"We just want to speak to you concerning an incident that took place some years ago, in Whitechapel," he quietly explained, holding both arms wide of his body, in a non-violent gesture. It would certainly have been interesting to see how he would have reacted if placed in the same position as Henry Bustle had been, in the Elephant and Jackal public house in The Irish Rookery.

Still the vagrant didn't speak and just stared at the two men who had accosted him, not realising they had afforded him the opportunity to put something inside his stomach before taking away his liberty, which they were about to do.

Another, smaller man, who was obviously one of the officials working at the Shelter, approached the two policemen and asked if he could assist them.

"No," Rayner answered bluntly, "We are on police business, and this gentleman is about to come with us to Scotland Yard. Is that not so, Peter?"

The vagrant still appeared to be present only as a bystander, and he continued to keep his own counsel.

The Inspector grasped his arm, and only then did the suspect show any sign of resistance by pulling away.

That was the signal for Rayner to change tactic, and all thoughts of diplomacy and linguistic subtlety disappeared. A clenched fist was quickly and effectively planted into Peter's mid-rift, causing the man to double over, before he was quickly hustled out through the front door, groaning and incoherently complaining of the way he was being treated. So much for diplomatic skills replacing brutality, and by the time the three men had reached the carriage awaiting them just a few streets away, their prisoner had slipped on the ice more than once, and had retreated back behind his previous wall of silence.

At least the interview room at Scotland Yard was warm, and Rayner instructed Jack Robinson to fetch a hot meal for the prisoner, deliberately doing so in the vagrant's presence, as an inducement for the man to converse with him.

"And bring back three mugs of tea Jack," he called after the young constable.

Turning to the other man, whose presence was noticeable from the stench coming from his person, the Inspector told him to stand, while he reluctantly and briefly searched him. After removing a glass bottle filled with some kind of clear spirit, and placing the same on the table, he asked his suspect for his name.

"You know who I am," the man answered, speaking with a slurred voice that could hardly be understood.

"You are the one they call Peter the Tinman?" Rayner asked, sitting opposite the itinerant with both hands clasped before him, as he leant across the table, "I need to know your real name."

"Tinman will do," the man said, "I do not know my real name. Why am I here, I haven't done anything?" Considering Peter had seemingly spent most of his life living on the streets of London, he appeared to be fairly lucid.

"I want you to think back to a time when you used to visit Turner Street and Mount Street a few years ago. Do you recall knowing two elderly sisters that used to keep a Tripe Shop on the corner there?"

"They was good to me," Peter confirmed, "They used to give me leftovers and hot tea."

"Left overs?"

"Old clothes and shoes and things to wear." He then reached inside his crumpled coat and produced an old tin plate with a fading portrait on the surface.

"One of them gave me this, and it's mine to keep."

Rayner could not conceal his surprise. It was a picture of what looked like a naval officer in uniform, wearing a peaked hat with some kind of badge on the front, which was unrecognisable.

"Can you remember which of the sisters' gave this to you, Peter?"

"The nice one who was fatter than the other one, although they were both nice ladies."

"Can you remember their names?"

"Barratt, that's all."

"Tell me the reason why you have kept this picture for so many years. It must be special to you?"

The vagrant shrugged his shoulders, before answering, "Not really. Nobody would buy it from me, so I just kept it, like this other one." He then reached inside the pocket of his trench coat and produced yet another tinplate, which was of a young lady, and was totally divorced from the Investigation being conducted.

Rayner was now beginning to understand how this man got his nickname, and asked who the lady in the picture was.

"I don't know. I found it in some garbage a long time ago and decided to keep it. It looked so lonely there, lying in the gutter."

"Going back to the two old dears who kept the Tripe Shop. Can you remember the last time you visited them?"

The tramp shook his head, and stared down at his worn boots, indifferently.

"Do you know the two women were killed fifteen years ago, in their home at that same address, where they kept the shop?"

"Yes."

"Did you kill them, Peter?" Rayner asked the question pointedly, and looked closely at the man's eyes, needing to measure his response.

Peter's eyes remained transfixed on his boots, and he remained speechless for some time, before slowly lifting his head and replying, "Yes, I killed them."

The Inspector stood from his seat and with both hands in his pockets, walked towards the closed door. He turned and leant back against it, before asking the obvious question.

"Tell me Peter, how did you kill them?"

The other man's words began to spill out of his mouth quickly, and his eyes were finally lifted to look directly at the Inspector.

"I smashed their heads in."

"What did you use to smash their heads in with?"

Peter paused, before admitting, "I can't remember, but I did it."

"Why did you kill the old ladies, Peter?" Rayner asked, remaining calm and unmoved.

"It's the Devil when he comes to visit me. I can't control him and I have to do as he tells me."

"And it was the Devil who told you to kill those two sisters?"

"He told me and I bashed their heads in, and it was him who told me to do it."

"Why are you lying to me, Peter?"

"I'm not. It's the truth."

"So, tell me, what did you do after you murdered them?"

"What do you mean?"

"What did you do? Did you just walk out and leave, or look for something to steal?"

The man had to consider the question before answering, and then claimed, "I left."

"Which way did you leave; through the front door or the back door?" Rayner shot the question at him instantaneously.

"Through the front door."

"Well, we know for certain the killer left through the back door Peter, and he also stole a lot of money from one of the cupboard drawers," the Inspector lied. "Did you do that Peter?"

"Yes."

"How much money did you take from that drawer then?"

"I can't remember, but I'm not lying and I took the money," he answered, continuing to nod his head, after he'd finished answering the question.

Rayner knew the man was lying, but for whatever reason, the answer lay somewhere inside an extremely muddled and disturbed mind. He then asked if he could keep the tinplate of the naval officer, and again the prisoner nodded his agreement.

The Inspector needed to try and get the man back to reality and to remember what he did or saw on the day of the murders, but as every minute passed by, it seemed as if Rayner was trying to achieve the impossible. He wasn't happy when the door was suddenly flung open, and the interview was interrupted by a chastened Superintendent Frederick Morgan.

The senior man beckoned the Inspector from the room, and when both officers were standing in the outside corridor, Morgan broke the news.

"There's been another murder Richard, in Bermondsey. A woman who owns a dressmaking business in Abbey Street, has been found dead with her skull caved in."

Rayner was bemused by the declaration, and wondered what it had to do with him, as if he didn't already have his hands full with the current Investigation. He just looked quizzically at the Superintendent.

"The dead woman is named Rose Kinley, and she's the step sister of the two Barratt women."

Chapter Eight

Ernest Pembleton was a man of ample girth, and a head the size of which compared favourably with his rounded torso. His physical appearance didn't quite support his vivacious manner, but the Detective Sergeant was extremely animated.

By the time Richard Rayner arrived at the small dressmaker's shop in Abbey Street, Bermondsey, a small crowd had gathered outside the front door. Before actually stepping inside the premises, the Inspector favoured standing anonymously at the back of the group of locals, making his own brief observations.

The comments he overheard consisted of the usual gossip and banter expected from individuals who were just being inquisitive. But what if the killer had returned to satisfy some bizarre desire to watch the police proceedings? What if the same person had a weird innuendo, which included listening to what local residents were saying about his fatalistic work? That was the reason for Rayner's initial action. But the officer saw no one who looked strange or out of place amongst the observers, much to his disappointment. So, he eventually stepped through the front door to be welcomed by the man in charge of London's most recent murder.

Although a rank lower than the Inspector, Sergeant Pembleton's position as the investigating officer had already been confirmed by Scotland Yard.

"The Superintendent told me you'd be following in my footsteps, Inspector," the loudly spoken man with the ruddy complexion and a face with jowls down either side, jocularly remarked.

"I am only here to observe Ernest. We suspect there could be a link between this victim and a case I am dealing with at the moment."

"The two sisters in Mount Street. Yes, I've been reading about it. The press appear to have already written off your chances with that one sir, if you don't mind me saying so."

"Don't believe everything you read in the newspapers Sergeant. The Superintendent doesn't. So, what have you found out so far?"

Both men were standing just inside the shop area, which comprised of a small counter, behind which there were two sewing machines, and various reams of cloth, mostly manufactured from linen and silk. They were spread across the same table supporting the apparatus. The only other items of furniture visible were two wooden chairs.

Although Pendleton wasn't the kind of man who would be regarded as a possible confidante by Rayner, or could be trusted to be as reliable as Henry Bustle, the visiting Inspector was impressed by the manner in which he had already gone about his initial business. Most of the premises seemed to be well lit by the placement of several lanterns, and constables had been posted to both the front and rear of the building to keep away inquisitive individuals, including local reporters.

"The dead woman is forty-eight year old Rose Kinley who is a dressmaker, and has been living alone here for the past few years. Although the doctor hasn't arrived yet, I believe she's been dead for about three hours now and is lying on the floor in the back parlour."

Rayner was reluctant to place any time of death on a deceased person, without it having first been confirmed by a medical specialist.

"Who found her?" he asked.

"A young girl who works here as the dressmaker's assistant." Pendleton paused to glance at his pocket book, before continuing, "Maisy Dunchurch is the girl's name and Miss Kinley had sent her to Dobson's Hosiery in Smithfield to collect a small bale of cloth. When the girl arrived back here at about six past the clock, she found her employer's body in the back room."

"Well done Sergeant. You seem to have covered most requirements at this early stage of the Investigation," Rayner said, complimenting the man, "Now, show me our Miss Rose Kinley."

The Inspector followed the Sergeant who walked with a spring in his step, having just had his ego boosted by the compliment received from such a famous detective. He stopped at the door leading to the parlour to allow, Rayner access.

From his initial observations of the body lying on a bloodstained mat, just in front of a grating in which there were still some smoldering coals, the victim was a small, petite lady, with long dark brown hair that was showing threads of grey. She lay on her back with both legs stretched out and her head was turned to one side. It was obvious a great deal of blood had come from a vicious looking wound on the back of her head, but there were other features which drew Rayner's attention. A number of slight bruises around her neck were visible, similar to those found around the throat of Emily Barratt. In fact, the room was uncannily similar to that in which the sisters had been found at the Mount Street address. The Inspector felt as if he was revisiting the same murder scene.

Could it be, the killer of fifteen years ago had struck again? Such a thought was in the back of Rayner's mind, although he would need conclusive proof that such was the case.

"I understand the lady was related to the sisters in Whitechapel," Rayner remarked, addressing the Sergeant whilst continuing to study the corpse.

"Yes Inspector. According to the young girl who worked here, she was their step sister."

"How would the girl know that Sergeant?"

"Apparently, and again according to Maisy Dunchurch, Rose Kinley used to visit her sisters' occasionally when they were alive, and used to tell her assistant how they would sit and share stories about their past lives together." Again, the Sergeant paused to consult his notes, before continuing, "Rose's husband, Bartram Kinley was alive in those days, but died a few years back of the Consumption. It was then that the victim opened this shop."

"You say that Rose was the Barratt ladies step sister, which would mean that she had the same father, Bartholomew?"

"It appears that was the case, but I still need to make further enquiries to confirm that."

"I see," Rayner confessed, wondering how many more of Emily and Gertrude Barratt's relatives were going to come to light during his own Investigation, "Have we any idea whether the business was a lucrative one or not?"

"Now that, I cannot tell you at the moment, but I'm sure we shall be getting clearer information about the business, as we continue with the Inquiry."

Pendleton then stood and watched as Richard Rayner began to examine the room itself, giving some attention to a couple of pictures that were hanging from the walls. But there was nothing containing any naval interest, which the Inspector was looking for. During that initial examination, it appeared that nothing had been disturbed and when he eventually made his way into the rear kitchen, all he found was a plate containing a half-eaten sandwich.

"Do you think she was having her lunch when she was disturbed by the killer, Inspector?" the Sergeant enquired.

"Possibly Ernest, possibly. Do we know if the shop was open at the time the lady was killed?"

"I believe so. According to young Maisy, it never closed until seven o'clock each evening."

Rayner then found that the kitchen door leading out to the rear garden, and which again reminded him of the one in Mount Street, was bolted from the inside. Unlike the fifteen-year old murders, Rose Kinley's killer must have left the scene via the front door.

He then turned and retraced his steps, climbing the stairs that separated the parlour from the front of the shop. At the top he reached a small dark and unlit landing, with two rooms leading off it. One was obviously used as a store room, with various bales of cloth piled up in one corner, but showing no sign of having been disturbed.

The second room was the dead lady's bedroom, containing a single bed covered with made up linen sheets beneath an eiderdown displaying an elaborate floral pattern. There was a wardrobe in one corner, and a dressing table and mirror beneath the window. Everything inside that room was scrupulously tidy and clean, and yet again, there was nothing to indicate that any other person, except for the occupier, had been in there. He pulled open the drawers inside the dressing table, but found nothing more than various small items that most women would have stored away for safe keeping.

Rayner stood for a moment inside the bedroom, trying to reason why such an apparently self-disciplined and gentle lady would be the victim of such a foul atrocity. He felt a surge of pity for the victim, who had done no more than spend her life working hard and trying to hold her business together, at a time when many were failing miserably. The most disappointing aspect of his search was a failure to identify a motive for the murder, which was similar to the Mount Street murders. Why would anyone wish to take the life of a lady who was obviously respectable and caring?

When he returned to the ground floor, he found the Sergeant talking with one of the constables, near to the front door.

"One more thing Ernest," Rayner said, "Do we know yet whether Rose Kinley had any children?"

"I put that very question to Maisy sir, but she had no idea. Rose had never mentioned having any kids to her."

"Have you any thoughts on what the reason behind this dreadful killing could be?"

"Not yet sir, no. I'm not sure whether the victim had been interfered with, and I shall request that the doctor, when he arrives, looks into that."

"I doubt that she has, but do point out the marks around her neck Ernest. It appears on the surface that the lady was partially strangled before being bludgeoned to death. Are you making arrangements to have the garden searched?"

"Yes sir, but the back door was bolted from the inside."

"I take your point, but it's still possible the killer could have thrown the murder weapon through a window into the garden. That is one possibility you will have to eliminate." Rayner was doubtful that was the case, and suspected the killer had taken the murder weapon with him, as it appeared to have happened in the sisters' case.

"I will sir."

"I wish you well with the Investigation, and I might just need to converse with you again, perhaps later, once you have the full picture."

Rayner left the premises in Abbey Street and caught a cab back to Scotland Yard. The only positive similarity between the two murder scenes was the bruising to Rose Kinley's neck, and of course, the interior layout of the building in Mount Street and the one he had just visited. The most recent scene was strangely identical with the one fifteen years earlier, but the Inspector wasn't prepared to pay too much attention to that fact. However, Rayner had little doubt that the most recent murder was connected in some way to that of the Barratt sisters, which also told him that the killer in both instances could have been the same man.

By the time the cabbie had driven his horse drawn carriage into the back yard of the Police Headquarters, the Inspector was still pondering over the fact that there appeared to no motive for either incident. Neither of the crimes had resulted from a drunken husband coming home and beating his wife to death; or a thief forcing his way into premises and attacking the occupiers; or if it came to that, some poor soul who had lost his mind, in similar fashion to Peter the Tinman, and had committed a frenzied attack on his victim.

A motiveless murder was the most difficult to detect, but having acknowledged that fact, Rayner was also aware that such circumstances left only a few other options to consider. In these cases, the most obvious were usually of a domestic nature. It was also possible that money was involved, or rather the stealing or embezzling of a large amount of money. But again, if that scenario existed, he was convinced it would only be revealed from further, more probing enquiries being made into the backgrounds of the unfortunate women involved. There had to be a link somewhere in the antecedents of the murdered victims, and that was where he would have to concentrate his efforts from now on.

When he reached the corridor outside his office, he came across Frederick Morgan and Jack Robinson, both looking anxious and dismayed. They were standing outside the Superintendent's office and Rayner approached them, questioningly.

"There's been an incident," Morgan told him, "Our man has cut his own throat at the top of the stairs over there."

The Inspector took a step back in disbelief.

"How, why?"

"Young Robinson gave him that meal you ordered, and he was left in your office to fill his belly. Anyway, the next thing we heard was your man screaming his head off about God and the sins he had committed. He ran down here with a broken piece of plate in his hand and stopped at the top of the stairs. Before we could reach him, he slit his throat with the broken plate and fell down the stairs, bleeding to death."

"Didn't anybody try to help him?" a shocked Inspector asked.

"Of course, we bloody well did. What do you think we are? But by the time we reached him and the lads from downstairs realised what was happening, he'd gone to join his Maker and confess his sins."

The Inspector turned and slowly walked back to his own office, his mind filled with a cocktail of grief, sympathy and guilt, having left the vagrant alone and unattended. As he stepped through the door, he overheard Morgan call to the constable to put the kettle on.

Chapter Nine

Both, Morgan and Rayner attended Peter the Tinman's funeral, Scotland Yard having paid to at least ensure the vagrant had more than a pauper's funeral. It was the least that could be done for a man who had killed himself whilst in their custody and supposed care. Not surprisingly, they were the only mourners in attendance, apart from those who, for whatever bizarre reasons, never failed to miss a burial.

As the box wood coffin was lowered into the ground, Rayner postured on the kind of life the occupant had led. In similar circumstances for so many others, opportunities for advancement had been extremely scarce for Peter the Tinman, and the old vagrant had taken his own life as a result of a disturbed mind. The Inspector could not rid himself of a slight feeling of guilt, having left the man alone in his office, following his false confession to an atrocious crime. He was silently profuse in his apologies to the dead man.

Frederick Morgan picked up the signals, and as the two policemen slowly walked away from the graveside towards their carriage, he turned to his Inspector and claimed, "You were not responsible for his death Richard. He took that decision unilaterally, and no one could have stopped him."

Rayner nodded, and answered by asking, "How then, could such a poor soul, having to survive with so much complexity and confusion in his mental faculties, make such a decision?"

"God only knows, my friend."

Following the events of the previous evening, Jack Robinson left Scotland Yard after being dismissed at the end of that day's tour of duty by Inspector Rayner. As he stepped out to hail a cab, which would take him back to his mother's home where he lodged, and had done so since the passing of his father some two years previously, the snow began to fall yet again.

After waiting for a short time, talking to a constable on duty at the main gate to the Police Headquarters building, and without there being any sign of a cabbie, the young man decided to keep warm by walking home.

"Keep moving Jack," the constable on gate duty called after him, "If you stop, you're likely to freeze to death."

Robinson dismissed the comment with a wave of his arm, and continued to slowly make his way gingerly across the snow packed pavement, thinking only of the hot broth his mother would have waiting for him, in her small back to back terraced house.

Turning into Whitehall, the snow became heavier and as he trundled in the direction of Trafalgar Square, with his head bowed down against a fairly strong wind that was blowing freezing particles into his face, he failed to see the dark non-descript carriage slowly approaching from behind. Even as the vehicle pulled up alongside him, Jack's eyes remained transfixed on his feet, as he struggled to maintain some purchase on the slippery pavement.

Two men, both wearing masks, suddenly leapt from the carriage and a cosh came down hard on the young constable's head, sending him sprawling into the fallen snow and ice. Then a piece of rag was placed across his nose and mouth, causing Richard Rayner's protégé to immediately lapse into unconsciousness. His two attackers then quickly bundled their victim's limp body into the one-horse carriage, before it galloped its way along Whitehall, in the same direction Jack Robinson had been walking. The kidnapping had been successful, without there being one single witness to the bizarre event.

When, Morgan and, Rayner returned to Scotland Yard, having paid their final respects to Peter the Tinman, on the morning following Constable Robinson's demise, the Sergeant on the front desk, called the Superintendent over.

"There's a lady waiting for you in your office sir. Constable Jackson is with her and she seems to be very distressed."

"Who is she?" the Superintendent asked.

"She says she's Constable Robinson's mother sir and reckons that her son didn't return home last night and she hasn't heard from him since."

"Then somebody had better explain to the woman that there are occasions when young men take it upon themselves to rid their minds and bodies of all frustrations, and do so by spending the night in some harlot's bed," the Superintendent smirked, "That's what young Robinson has been up to, and I shall place his pride and joy into a vice before transforming it into something that resembles a fillet of Plaice, when he finally decides to turn up."

Frederick Morgan's jocularity didn't make much impression on his Inspector and Richard Rayner looked concerned, advising the senior detective that he himself had dismissed the absent constable the night before.

"I don't believe Jack Robinson is the kind of young man to whom you refer to, Superintendent and I fear that something foreboding might have happened to him."

"Good God man, don't be so naïve," Morgan snapped back, "He's a young man with a young man's urges in his loins, and the willingness to do something about it. That's all we need to know."

The two men found Mrs. Robinson sitting in a chair inside Morgan's office with a young constable doing his best to console her.

"What's this all about Mrs. Robinson?" Morgan loudly and abruptly asked of the lady.

"This is Superintendent Morgan, Mrs. Robinson and I am Inspector Rayner, who your son works for," the Inspector explained, in a much calmer voice than his senior, "We understand that Jack didn't come home last night."

The lady looked up at Rayner, ignoring the other detective and with reddened eyes explained, "I always expect Jack to be late because of his work, but he never stays out all night, and I kept his broth simmering until the early hours. I'm certain something has happened to him. I didn't want to bother you in case he'd been detained at work, but when there was no sign of him this morning, thought it best to inform you."

"You did the right thing my dear," Rayner confirmed, "But I am sure your son is okay. Jack can well look after himself. Now, I will get a constable to drive you home and we shall make a few enquiries to find your son. I'm sure there is nothing to worry about."

"What about lady friends?" Morgan blurted out, "I mean, the chances are that he's been waylaid by one of them, don't you think?"

"He doesn't have any girlfriends, Superintendent," the lady corrected the man whose office they were in, "He lives for his job."

"Well you know what young men are like, that's all I'm saying," the senior man remarked insensitively.

"Not my Jack, Superintendent, and I am not the kind of doting mother that is unaware of a young man's fancies, but I know my son and what you are implying, just doesn't make any sense."

After Mrs. Robinson had left in the company of Constable Jackson, Rayner suggested he should make a few enquiries to try and find out the last occasion the missing police officer was seen and by whom. However, the Superintendent was more optimistic that the young man would turn up with a hangover, after spending a night wallowing in debauchery.

"You cannot afford to leave the Barratt Investigation, Inspector," he pointed out, tenaciously, "If you are really worried about young Robinson, then I'll arrange for one of the other lads to make a few enquiries."

Rayner nodded his appreciation and left, intending to visit another missing member of his team, Henry Bustle, who he was hoping would be well on his way to recovery. He had been missing his old friend and colleague and could certainly have done with the man at his side at that particular moment, although he knew deep down, that was extremely unlikely.

When he arrived at the Bustle household, a small terraced house in Lambeth, he was greeted at the door by his Sergeant's wife, Nellie. She seemed to be flustered by the antics of their four children, who were aged between, four and eleven years. Their mother was a slim woman, having retained her youthful and attractive looks throughout many years of toil and hard work. In Rayner's opinion, Nellie Bustle was her husband's main support, having accepted the responsibility of rearing their four children virtually singlehandedly, and without ever making any complaint. The Inspector also knew that for his part, Henry Bustle loved his wife dearly, and felt he was the luckiest man in the world.

"Do come in Inspector," she warmly invited, opening the door wider for the visitor to enter, "He's in the front parlour, and will be glad to see you." She then turned and quickly scolded her oldest lad who was causing havoc, running up and down the stairs.

Rayner was surprised to see his Sergeant sitting in an armchair, up against a roaring log fire. Most of the swelling had gone down, helping to restore his scarred face to some kind of normal ugliness, and the bruises that had distorted his features were also beginning to fade.

The Inspector smiled as he took a seat opposite the man of the house.

"I must admit you look a lot better than the other day, Henry. How are you feeling now?"

"Apart from my ribs, there's nothing wrong with me, thanks to some old fashioned remedies off the wife, and three days of boredom. I cannot wait to get back sir. How are things going? Have we made much progress with the murders?"

Rayner described the second murder of Rose Kinley to him, and made mention of the possible link to the sisters' Investigation. He also briefly told Bustle of the events surrounding the arrest of Peter the Tinman, and the Sergeant was surprised when told of the suicide.

"What about the nautical connection we came across?" Henry Bustle asked.

"We might have a picture of the man we are seeking," the Inspector told him, enthusiastically. He then went on to describe the way in which the vagrant had produced the tin plate, and gave it to his Sergeant to scrutinise.

"Before he took his own life, the Tinman swore that Gertrude Barratt had given it to him, although he rudely referred to her as being the fatter of the two ladies."

"Do you believe him?"

"No, it's more likely he stole it, but I'm convinced it came from the shop in Mount Street, and that being the case, there is every possibility he must be the same naval officer who Charlie Walker mentioned, who was present when he followed Emily Barratt into the parlour on the day before the sisters were killed."

"That seems a reasonable assumption, but how are you going to trace the man in this picture? It must have been taken years ago."

"If only we had known about the existence of the two ladies step sister Rose Kinley, before she was murdered," Rayner complained, "I need to make some further enquiries to trace any other relatives who were close to the sisters."

"That should have been picked up by Albert Greening during the initial enquiries he and his merry men were supposed to have made. I'll tell you what, give me a jiffy and I will come with you," the Sergeant intimated, standing from his chair, only to wince in searing pain.

"You're not ready yet Henry, to come bounding around the streets of London. It looks like you will need a few more days yet for those ribs to heal."

The patient nodded, and slowly returned to the comfort of his chair.

"At least young Robinson is there to help you. How is he doing by the way?"

"I'm afraid he's gone missing." Rayner then explained about the visit of Jack Robinson's mother to Scotland Yard that morning, and confirmed the young constable hadn't been seen since the evening before, when he left work to go home.

"Well, I'll be damned."

"Superintendent Morgan seems to think the lad has spent a night indulging himself in lust and fornication."

"I doubt that, not Jack Robinson."

"So does his mother."

It was daylight when the young constable finally regained consciousness, and immediately felt as if his arms were on fire. Through the light coming in from a slit of a window in one wall, it appeared he was in some kind of large shed, and from the smell that teased his nostrils, it had been used recently as a store room. The odour of soap and other detergents was strong, although not much was visible in the poor light.

Both of his wrists were bound tightly to a beam above his head, and his toes were just about touching the wooden floorboards. He had also been stripped down to his waist and felt as though his accommodation was an ice box, unable to prevent the muscular spasms that were dominant throughout his upper naked body.

The young constable's face was distorted by the throbbing pain coming from his arms, and he quickly glanced around his confinement, recognising the outline of a number of boxes piled up in one far corner. There was a door immediately in front of him and a small stool to his left. Jack cried out to anyone who could hear him, but there was no response and the discomfort now wracking his torso, made it difficult for the young man to think clearly. He did realise however, that if he was to escape from his incarceration, he needed to clear his mind, and quickly.

His head felt as if someone was trying to pound the back of his skull to gain entrance, and he tried to concentrate on remaining absolutely still, until his mind began to clear; but it was hopeless.

Looking up, he could see that both his wrists had been secured by pieces of hemp, which were cutting into his skin and adding to the pain he was feeling elsewhere. He tried hard to think logically but couldn't. The young man was at the mercy of those who had kidnapped and drugged him, before hanging him up like a shot Pheasant.

Once again, he screamed out as best he could, "Is anyone there. Can you please help me," but no one came, and he wished he hadn't regained consciousness.

Chapter Ten

"Good morning Inspector."

Richard Rayner immediately stood from behind his desk, surprised to see none other than the Commissioner standing there, with Superintendent Morgan behind him.

Sir Edmund Henderson was a well built, former Royal Engineers officer, who had previously held a number of senior management positions in Canada and New Brunswick, before returning to England. He was a distinguished looking gentleman, immaculately dressed with dark grey hair and mutton chop whiskers that met over the top of a full mouth.

Although preferring to remain on his feet, he beckoned the Inspector to return to his seat, and immediately asked about the news regarding the missing officer, Constable Robinson.

Rayner looked directly at Frederick Morgan and answered with all due diligence, "As far as I am aware, he is still missing, sir."

"Yes," the Superintendent confirmed, "As I said upstairs, it's a mystery sir. The lad left here on that particular night and hasn't been seen since."

"So, what have we done so far to track him down Inspector?" the Commissioner asked Rayner directly.

"I apologise sir," Rayner openly admitted, "I do not have personal knowledge of the details, because unfortunately I have been involved in the Investigation of the double murder of the two sisters' in Whitechapel fifteen years ago. But I do know a number of enquiries have been conducted in an effort to trace Constable Robinson's whereabouts, but so far without there having been any success."

It was the answer Sir Edmund had anticipated, and the Head of the Metropolitan Police turned to Frederick Morgan and explained in an authoritative voice, "The recovery of Constable Robinson has to be top priority Frederick, and might I suggest we need our best detective officer to be involved in the hunt for this missing officer."

"Yes of course, sir."

"The Case Review of the two ladies unfortunate deaths has waited fifteen years to be resolved, it can wait a little longer, but we need to find that officer and quickly."

"I shall see to it sir, that Inspector Rayner gives the matter his complete attention," the Superintendent answered uncomfortably, and obviously feeling like a schoolboy who had just been indirectly chastised.

Although, Rayner was delighted to be able to pick up the reins of what he regarded as a serious missing person Inquiry, he also felt some disappointment at having to put the Barratt sisters' Investigation on hold temporarily. Of course, he was concerned about Jack Robinson's sudden disappearance, but had felt at that moment, he was finally beginning to make some progress with the historical case.

"How are you getting on with that Investigation by the way?" the Commissioner asked, with genuine interest.

"There has been some progress sir, and I feel that we are finally getting closer to identifying the killer."

"Excellent. I shall inform the newspapers of that optimism Inspector. They are beginning to create some disquiet amongst the populace with extremely critical and damning reports of what we have been doing. I am sure you will be happy to give them some positive news Frederick."

"Most certainly, sir," the Superintendent answered, again realising it was his responsibility to answer to the press.

"I am to meet with the Home Secretary later this afternoon, and I shall explain that we have made considerable progress in the case. Can I assume an arrest is imminent?" he asked, turning back to Richard Rayner.

"No sir, it would be wrong to assume an arrest is imminent," the Inspector retorted, "But I am confident of being in a position very soon, when I can name the person responsible." Rayner was confident that his words spoke the truth.

Although obviously disappointed with his junior officer's reply, Sir Edmund smiled and nodded his understanding. At least Rayner had been honest with him, and he was now aware of the reality of the Inspector's efforts.

"Carry on Inspector," the Commissioner said, before turning to leave with the Superintendent, "And find that missing officer as a matter of urgency."

"Yes sir."

After the two senior officers had departed, Richard Rayner sat at his desk for some time, pondering over the options he should consider to undertake an initial start to a man hunt involving Jack Robinson's unusual disappearance. Too much time had been wasted already, and the Inspector would approach his new task with both determination and a great deal of urgency. The one problem he was aware of, was that the man he knew would have been in a position to assist greatly, was unfortunately still recovering from a beating sustained in the Irish Rookery in St Giles in the Field. Rayner quietly cursed Henry Bustle for having subjected himself to what he regarded as having been self-inflicted injuries.

Bustle had received a Baptism of Fire when, as a young recruit he had been posted to the same district as a patrolling officer. Yet being the kind of bobby who would stand for no nonsense and take on whatever the locals threw at him, he had earned a great deal of respect amongst the inhabitants of the patch known as, The Holy Land. His informants in that quarter were numerous, and there was little the Sergeant couldn't find out about, when required to do so. Unfortunately, the most recent beating laid at his doorstep went with the territory.

Rayner left his office and made his way downstairs to the public reception area, where he approached the desk sergeant, a colossus of a man who sported a large grey walrus moustache, which partially hid a badly scarred face. He was one of many who carried the scars of having spent years policing the streets in Victorian London.

"Frank, have you any idea of who young Jack Robinson's closest friend was, when he walked the beat?" the Inspector asked.

"That's a difficult one sir," the Sergeant answered, "He was a popular lad," he continued, speaking as though the constable was dead, "But I suppose if anybody was really close to him, it was young Willie Collins. He knew Robinson better than most I suppose. He's on duty now and due to come in for his break. Shall I send him up to you Inspector?"

"Please do, Frank. I shall be in my office."

Jack Robinson felt as though he was facing the Grim Reaper full on; he was that close to opening death's door. Both arms had gone numb with all the blood having been drained from them, but his real problem was the intense cold, and he constantly shivered violently. The young man had been left unattended for a long time without food or water, and was beginning to accept he had been left trussed up in that lonely storeroom, to end his days there in the most painful and traumatic way.

Both Jack's throat and mouth were parched, and his ability to call out had long left him. Although the thumping inside his head had subsided, his teeth chattered and every ounce of willingness to live had abandoned him. He was still hanging there, having accepted his fatal end, when the sound of the bolts being slid from the other side of the wooden door, brought him out of his tortuous apathy.

He opened his eyes and tried to speak, but couldn't.

A man, small in stature and wearing a mask, entered the room and quickly stepped across the dirt floor before cutting the constable down, causing him to fall to the ground, but leaving his wrists still bound together. No words were spoken and the man then placed a blindfold over Jack's eyes, before placing a blanket around his shoulders. It was an unexpected gesture of kindness, for which Jack was appreciative.

The prisoner could hear his goaler breathing, and became aware of a second man entering the room. He was given sips of water and a piece of dried bread was placed in his hands, which he quickly began to gnaw away at. Was it possible he was about to be released? His optimism was short lived.

"Don't get too heartened by all of this," A rasping voice echoed in his ear, "We are only keeping you alive to kill you when the time is right Jack, my old friend."

"Why?" the constable gasped, managing to find his voice, as he chewed on the stale bread and sipped more of the water from the bowl that had been left at his side, "Who are you?"

"Your worst nightmare Jack Robinson," the disguised voice continued, "You are going to die here mate, but not before we have paid you back for your sins of yesteryear."

Jack's mind became tormented and he begged his captors to release the bonds tying his wrists together, as both his hands and arms felt as if they were stuck in the middle of a raging furnace. His upper limbs were covered in dried blood, a result of the ropes cutting into his flesh. But his pleas were in vain, as he heard the door close and the bolts on the outside being replaced. At least he had been shown some mercy, no matter how small.

Constable William Collins was a tall, dangly young man, with long brown unkempt hair, and a face covered in pimples which made him look more of an adolescent than a mature man who had the responsibility of patrolling a beat in London.

"Come in Willie," Rayner warmly greeted the young man, "I understand you are a close friend of Jack Robinson's?"

"I was sir, when we walked the beat together, but I haven't seen Jack so much these days, since he joined the Detective Branch."

"You appreciate, Willie, that Jack has been missing for a day or two now, and I was wondering if you could help us to find him."

"I will try sir."

"What I'm looking for is some information about his background, such as who might have abducted him, or even worse, harmed him in some way."

"I don't know of anybody who would do that to Jack, sir." Constable Collins wasn't the brightest man in the Metropolitan Police, and certainly not the kind of individual who could suddenly project some innovative idea, aimed towards remedying a problem. But, he was an honest soul, and would do all he could to help out a mate.

Rayner was aware of those qualities in the lad, and was hoping that, even unwittingly, the young man might provide some information which would be a starting point towards finding out what had happened to Constable Robinson.

"Tell me Willie, do you know of any lady friends Jack might have had in the past, or perhaps someone to whom he owed money?"

The other man smiled insincerely, and explained, "He wouldn't borrow money sir. He was always condemning the Money Lenders as being sharks, but he did have a couple of lady friends I remember he mentioned."

"Any lady in particular?"

"I'm not sure if I should mention this sir. Jack did tell me in confidence."

"Willie if there is anything out of the ordinary connected with Jack Robinson, I need to know. He could well be lying somewhere at this moment, seriously wounded or perhaps dead, so speak up man."

"Can I speak to you in confidence, and close the door please sir?"

Rayner hadn't noticed that the young man had left the door to his office open after first stepping into the room, and nodded his consent.

"Speak up lad," he demanded, after watching a very nervous Willie Collins ensure that no one else was privy to their conversation.

"Just before he came to work with you sir, Jack used to walk the beat in the Kensington Road, close to Lambeth Road, when I patrolled the next beat to him." The young constable paused, and allowed his eyes to drop down, staring at the piece of mat spread out across the Detective Inspector's highly polished floor.

"Go on Willie," Rayner prompted, encouraging the man to continue, which was as tedious as drawing teeth, but remaining patient, knowing that Constable Collins was about to breach a trust placed in him by his friend and colleague.

"Well sir, Jack met this girl see, who was a barmaid at one of the local public houses. He seemed to be stricken by the wench and went with her for a few weeks, or it might have been several months." Again, Collins stopped speaking.

"Go on Willie."

"Well sir, one day we was talking, having met up at a point where our two beats met, and he told me the girl had become pregnant, and he was worried what her brothers would do to him, once they found out."

"How long ago did this happen Willie?"

"It must have been a few months ago now, sir."

"Do we know the girl's name?"

"I met her once, when she was arm in arm with Jack, walking across Westminster Bridge. Her name was Lizzie, but I never caught her second name. She was a little girl with short dark hair and well blessed for her size sir, if you know what I mean?"

"Obviously Jack thought the same."

"Yes sir."

"Do you know the public house where this girl worked?"

"The Plume of Feathers in North Street."

"Thank you Willie. You have been a great help."

"Will this stay between us, Inspector?" the young man asked, obviously concerned by what he had just shared with the Detective Inspector.

"I can't guarantee that lad, but you won't be in any trouble, I can assure you of that."

As the constable turned to leave, there was a knock on the door, and Willie opened it. Much to Richard Rayner's elation, Henry Bustle was standing there with a look of anticipation across his face.

"Welcome back Henry. It's so bloody good to see you again."

"Is there anything I can help you with Inspector?"

"More than I can say my old friend, but only on one condition. You refrain from getting involved in any more street fights, until we have sorted out the cases of the double murder and missing constable."

Chapter Eleven

Henry Bustle's early return to duty was a determining boost for Richard Rayner, who appreciated the chances of solving the fifteen year old enigma concerning the double murder in Whitechapel, had now doubled. However, the Detective Inspector remained concerned about his Sergeant's indubitable fitness, suspecting his friend's enthusiasm might be concealing some irritating physical weaknesses. But for now, Bustle's valuable presence would undoubtedly assist Rayner's own confidence and concentration. Of course, before they could proceed further with the Case Review, it was imperative they quickly traced the whereabouts of the missing Jack Robinson.

The Inspector was also aware that, what appeared to have been a major troublesome event, creating the one blemish on the missing constable's personal history, was in reality, the strongest lead he had been given yet. They had to find the girl Lizzie, who had the misfortune of having become pregnant, supposedly following a romantic association with the young man from Scotland Yard. At least, Richard Rayner now had a realistic and promising starting point for his endeavour to return the missing constable to the fold, and relieve the anxieties being afforded his mother in particular.

The two detectives discussed the need to visit The Plume of Feathers public house in North Street, Lambeth, where the girl had apparently worked as a barmaid. Bustle put forward his own suggestion. He proposed that it would be more expedient if he visited the premises in person, rather than expose his Inspector who, in his usual refinery and silk top hat, would be more likely to attract sniggers and jibes, rather than valuable information.

Such a submission was not regarded in anyway as a personal affront by Rayner, and the Inspector recognised the logic behind the suggestion, before agreeing wholeheartedly that the Sergeant should take on that particular mission. Although Richard Rayner was no stranger to the seedier life on the streets of London, his main strength lay in his ability to analyse situations, and deploy various strategies that were appropriate to divaricating circumstances. On the other hand, his Sergeant had amassed sufficient experience by mingling with the lower classes throughout his life. He had proved constantly that he had the distinction of being one of their most understanding members.

The Inspector required some time in which he could complete a record of the intelligence upon which he was about to act, and the two men agreed to meet in North Street within the hour. Henry Bustle had already left Rayner's office, when he was unexpectedly confronted by none of other than, Superintendent Frederick Morgan, in the outside corridor.

"Well, the Prodigal Son appears to have returned to the fold," the Superintendent jocularly commented, on seeing the Sergeant.

Bustle just nodded in acknowledgement.

"No more fisty cuffs with half the bloody Irish Nation Henry; understand lad?"

"There were only four of them last time sir, and I would have got the better of them if they hadn't surprised me," he lied, laughing as he descended the stairs to return to the streets of London. The Detective Sergeant intended putting the time he had prior to the rendezvous with his Inspector to good use, calling on a number of his informants to test their knowledge regarding the whereabouts of the missing constable.

In fact, by the time Henry Bustle finally arrived at the Plume of Feathers public house, he was late, having had no joy with his additional and diversionary enquiries. Slightly embarrassed, he quickly discovered his more affluent looking Inspector Rayner had been waiting at the same location for a good twenty minutes.

"Sorry sir, this won't take a jiff," he half apologetically said to his senior detective, popping his head through the open window of the waiting carriage.

"Take care Henry and avoid any confrontation," Rayner sincerely advised, obviously more concerned about his Sergeant's health than his lateness.

Surprisingly, the Sergeant was gone for only a few minutes and when he returned, there was a look of jubilation on his face, which was still showing the signs of his more recent violent altercation.

"I know this girl," he confessed, "Or at least I know of her family, which include Lizzie's two brothers, James and Shaun Donogue. They both work off a meat stall in Smithfield Market, and I can tell you that you will not meet two bigger mischief makers than that pair."

Before joining the Metropolitan Police, Henry Bustle had himself worked in his family's butchery business, and it was during that period he got to know most other people involved in the same trade as a matter of course, including the two Donogue brothers.

After jumping into the carriage to sit beside the Inspector, the Sergeant continued to explain that both men he was referring to were Irish, as hard as the nails used to keep boots on their feet.

"They were known to deal in cheap meat, brought across from Ireland and sold to Londoners at much cheaper prices than the rest of us could afford. In fact, their antics put a few smaller butchers out of business," he continued, "And their willingness to dish out one or two beatings in return for payment, was an enjoyable side line for them."

"Do we know where they live, Henry?"

"In Whitechapel, but I think I know exactly where they would be keeping Jack Robinson, if those two are responsible for kidnapping him. But a word of caution Inspector. I would not put it beyond them to have already sent young Jack to meet his Maker, if their blood was up."

"Where were you thinking of?" Rayner asked, impatiently.

"Well, close to the market in Smithfield there are a few store rooms used by various meat dealers, which are packed with ice and where large quantities of meat are stored, before being offered for sale to the punters. I think that's where we should start looking."

"Well done Henry, but this time I think it would be wise to take a few precautions, before we go airing in, and I do believe this is one you should absent yourself from."

Bustle pouted his mouth, but accepted the Inspector's advice was a sensible precaution.

"Back to the Yard then, is it?"

Rayner nodded, and called to the driver of the carriage to return to Police Headquarters.

Jack Robinson was a frightful sight, crouched in a corner beneath the narrow window, which was far too small for him even to think about escaping through, even if he had the strength and will power to do so. He was wrapped in the blanket given him by one of his kidnappers, but couldn't stop every muscle in his body from twitching in the freezing temperature in which he had been forced to remain.

His upper garments had been removed from the store room completely, and although he could see a piece of hessian sacking resting across a beam above his head, the young constable hadn't the strength or ability to attempt to grab the item, not that it would have helped in anyway. The only thing that could have, would have been a fur coat and open fire.

He heard the door being unbolted again, as his teeth continued chattering and looked up in surprise when two men stepped inside, but on this occasion, neither of them was hiding their faces behind masks. In Jack's confused mind, as far as he was concerned, that could only mean one thing. They had returned to kill him and that could be the only reason why the men weren't worried that he could recognise them at a later date. It wouldn't be important to them, if he was a corpse.

One of the men was smaller than the other, and had an oval face with light blue eyes that pierced through their prisoner's concentration. He was also thinner than the other man, but looked just as aggressive.

The second man was much bigger than the first, with curly red hair and a bushy moustache. Both men were wearing heavy clothing, and the second, larger sized assailant, had a band of gold hanging from one ear.

"Up," the red head demanded, kicking their prisoner in his side and causing him to groan.

The shivering wretch tried, but couldn't force himself to leave the dirt floor, so was helped by the red head, who grabbed the blanket from him and violently yanked him up by his hair, until his shivering carcass had straightened up. He then forced Jack's bound hands back on to the beam above his head, pulling his body in an upward direction, until he was returned to the same position he had found himself when first regaining consciousness, following his abduction. The blanket that had undoubtedly prevented him from freezing to death was discarded. Dressed only in his trousers, the captive hung there, still shivering as though being slowly and tortuously dragged back towards the brink of death once again.

"We haven't been introduced," the smaller of the two men then said, speaking in a broad Irish accent, "I'm Shaun Donogue and this is my brother Jimmy. We are Lizzie Donogue's brothers."

Jack shook his head and tried to speak, but couldn't.

"Did you know that you were the father of a bouncing boy, you fornicating bastard, and our little sister is in despair, thanks to you."

The man's voice was distant to the poor soul hanging from the beam, but Jack could still make out every word being spoken. If there had been any doubt before, that his life was about to end, such a sliver of optimism now disappeared.

"So, in return for you lumbering our sister with a bastard child, we thought it would be appropriate if you paid her back for having refused to do the honourable thing, by sacrificing your life for her. Would you agree?"

Still, Jack shook his head without having the ability to make any verbal protests. These two bullying reprobates weren't playing games, and their unfortunate victim was well aware they would carry out their threats.

The bigger of the two brothers then produced a heavy chain of steel, and held it in one hand, before proclaiming, "We are going to give you a taste of what we do to fornicating bastards like you, back home in the Emerald Isle."

The chain menacingly rattled as it was dragged across the floor, within striking distance of the suspended victim.

"First, I'm going to break both of your kneecaps boy. Then your elbows, and when you're writhing in agony and begging me to stop, guess what. I'm going to crush your skull with this," he threatened, deliberately shaking the heavy piece of chain.

Jack closed his eyes in surrender. What could he do? There was no escape and he realised these two Irish bully boys had made him suffer so badly, death would be his only salvation. And even after keeping him in such freezing conditions for all of that time, they were intent on causing him more pain, before finally taking his life. For what? Jack asked himself. Because he had refused to enter into a lifelong loveless marriage with a girl he'd known only for a few weeks. For one singular mistake they had both made when driven by lust for a short, momentary demonstration of consequential irresponsibility.

The chain struck him behind both knees, creating explosions of pain that ran through his whole body, and he screamed out in excruciating agony.

The red headed man who had inflicted the first blow grinned, relishing the moment, and obviously reveling in his role as a masochistic torturer. These two weren't normal people and obviously wallowed in administering agony to others.

For the first time since his confinement, Jack Robinson felt sweat running down his brow. His face was pale and he felt nauseated from the damage already inflicted by his tormenter's weapon; the heavy chain which was now being positioned in readiness for yet another blow, which Jack believed would in all probability bring an end to his life. His heart would not be able to cope with a repeat of the same intense pain he had just already experienced.

"That was for our sister," the red head claimed, "And this is for the baby boy you were so willing to abandon."

As his arm came up the door to the store room suddenly burst open, and a body of policemen burst in, led by Richard Rayner.

Before either man could respond, both were clubbed to the ground with the bigger of the two offering some resistance, but unable to prevent a state of unconsciousness resulting from multiple blows to his head from a number of hard wooden truncheons. The brothers' playtime was at an end, and thankfully for the human toy with which they were so gamely inflicting their own brand of misery on, they had failed to achieve their version of finality.

Rayner immediately cut Jack Robinson down, who was still grimacing from the violent treatment he had received, and without further consideration, grabbed a heavy coat off one of the prisoners before throwing it over the injured constable's shoulders. The Inspector could see that his former protégé was in dire need of medical attention, and as the two Irish butchers were taken off in carriages back to Scotland Yard, young Jack was quickly transported to the nearest hospital.

Sergeant Bustle had watched the whole incident from a stationary carriage outside, having been forbidden to take part in the arrests by Richard Rayner, the latter having not wanted to risk any further injury to his colleague. But he was allowed to visit the girl who was at the centre of Jack Robinson's abduction and torture, together with his Inspector.

Having satisfied themselves that Lizzie Donogue was completely unaware of what atrocities had taken place, the two detectives left her, after assuring the girl she would not be put in the dock with her two brothers. But the greatest satisfaction came when they visited Jack's mother to inform her that her son had been found safe, if not entirely well.

When they later saw Constable Robinson lying in a warm hospital bed, they were both surprised to see how much the young man had recovered, with colour back in his cheeks and a smile across his face. His ordeal was over; an ordeal which had seen him facing the end of life itself, and young Jack couldn't thank the two detectives enough for having saved his life.

As they both left the hospital, Richard Rayner turned to his Sergeant and quietly suggested, "Perhaps now, Henry, we can get on with the real business of solving a murder." There was work to do, and the detectives headed back to Scotland Yard to re-new their efforts and concentration on finding the killer of the two Barratt sisters.

Chapter Twelve

Henry Bustle followed the prison guard down a number of corridors, frequently having to pause and wait for his escort to unlock various gates, before passing through. The solid floors all appeared to be covered with straw and the Sergeant wondered whether he was actually inside a Prison, or visiting a stable maintained for horses. Finally, he was directed into a small windowless room behind yet another locked door, and asked to sit in one of two chairs either side of a small table.

After a few minutes, the door opened again and the man Bustle was visiting, appeared in the company of another Prison Guard.

Royston Whittle was a forty-year old man, small and thin with dark hair cut short, obviously by the prison barber, considering the uneven patches of hair around his cranium. His hazel eyes were like two small beads of glass sunken inside a ferret-like face, but the noticeable identification mark that had helped the Sergeant convict the man of robbing a Mail train some five years earlier, was a tattoo of a serpent on the back of his right hand.

When initially being dealt with by Henry Bustle, Whittle had covertly helped the Sergeant in identifying the other members of the gang, but had still been sentenced to twenty years Hard Labour. Since his imprisonment, the convicted criminal had provided various snippets of useful information to the detective, in return for packets of tobacco. Richard Rayner's right hand man was hoping he would have similar success yet again.

The small chain attached to both the prisoner's ankles rattled, as he took a seat opposite his visitor, with the guard remaining inside the room, casually leaning against the wall adjacent to the only door.

"How's it going, Roy?" Bustle enquired, starting the conversation with the usual rapport.

"As you see me Mr. Bustle," the man quietly answered.

"Then you look well my friend, except for that quilted hair cut inflicted on you."

Whittle just nodded with a smile lacking humour, surprisingly not making any comment on the blemishes that still marked his visitor's face.

"Roy, I want you to cast your mind back to fifteen years ago in Whitechapel, when two elderly sisters were murdered at their shop in Mount Street, on the corner of Turner Street."

"I remember Mr. Bustle. Didn't they own a Tripe Shop or something like that?"

"That's right, and the reason I've come to see you is to ask for some help. Can you remember what was said about it on the streets at the time?"

The prisoner shook his head, before explaining, "Only what I've just told you."

"There must have been some talk amongst the villains you mixed with in the area, or perhaps when you were all meeting to plan how to knock over that Mail train."

"No, nothing more. We had other things on our minds at that time," he offered, now smiling genuinely.

"What about any general chat in here amongst the inmates. Have you overheard any remark or opinion that might be of some help to me?"

"Nothing."

"Roy, both you and me know only too well that prison restricts your movements, but it also sharpens ears." As he spoke, the Sergeant stretched out an arm across the table top with a clenched fist.

Whittle knew the well-rehearsed sign, and quickly covered the fist with his own tattooed hand, before snatching a packet of tobacco from Bustle's palm. The item disappeared in a flash, and the detective glanced across at the guard standing by the door, who was still standing in the same position, looking but not really seeing with his mind obviously elsewhere.

The Sergeant's informant leant forward and lowering his voice, admitted, "There was some talk on the streets at the time that the old women had been done in, as a result of some initiation ceremony by one of the local gangs in Whitechapel, and I've heard the same being spoken by one or two of the blokes in here."

"Was that a rumour, or a fact?"

The chained prisoner shrugged his shoulders with an indifferent look on his face.

"Okay Roy, what was the name of the gang?"

"The Brick Lane Ratters. They were a band of small-time crooks led by an overgrown dickhead by the name of, Black Jake Quarry, who lived in Osborn Place, just around the corner from Brick Lane."

The Sergeant's initial assessment of what his informant was disclosing was dubious, and yet the man had never lied to him before. The tale given was worthy of further probing.

"What's this gambit about some initiation ceremony then, Roy?"

"Every time they recruited a new kid to the gang Mr. Bustle, they gave him a test to pass, know what I mean? Word had it, this new member was ordered to kill somebody so he could be accepted into the gang. According to the gossip, together with Black Jake, the kid got into the Tripe Shop somehow and murdered the two old dears."

Henry Bustle looked straight into the prisoner's eyes for a brief moment, and then declared, "I think you're giving me a load of bollocks, Roy."

"Well, you asked me Mr. Bustle and I've only told you only what I heard."

At the same time the Sergeant was visiting Royston Whittle in prison, Richard Rayner was returning to Portsmouth, still enjoying the satisfaction of having reunited Jack Robinson with the loving care of his mother, as the train careered southwards. By the time he arrived at the Harbour Railway Station for the second time in as many weeks, dusk was approaching and he was tempted to book a room for the night, before paying a visit to the man he intended to see. However, there was always a risk that if he left it much later, the Master at Arms might have finished for the day and retired to his habitat.

The Inspector found, Elias Gardiner crouched over his desk, studying some charts by the light of a tallow candle. The experienced naval officer looked surprised when Rayner entered his office, after first tapping on the door.

"Well Inspector, what brings you back at this late hour sir?" Gardiner asked, folding up the chart he had been scrutinising.

"Something perhaps not as interesting as you appear to be engaged with," Rayner commented, staring down at the array of charts on the desk top.

The Master smiled, obviously pleased that his visitor was showing some interest in his unusual work.

"We have to maintain various measurements on land masses, as well as ocean depths," he explained enthusiastically, "And it has fallen upon me to compare the current position of the coastline running down the South East of England with measurements taken some ten years ago."

"And out of interest, have you found any variation?"

"Oh yes, we always do and it appears this time we have lost over a foot of land to the sea, since this part of the country was last surveyed."

Rayner nodded his appreciation of the knowledge shared, and remarked, "Erosion of the coast on the Eastern shores, but perhaps we might have regained the same loss on the opposite side of the country?"

"That is likely, but we shall have to see. So, I am sure you haven't called to assess one of the many duties for which I am responsible."

"You are correct sir." The Inspector produced the tinplate given him by Peter the Tinman, and handed it to the naval officer.

"I realise it's a long shot, but I was hoping you might be able to identify the officer in this picture."

Elias Gardiner moved the tallow candle closer to the tinplate and sat studying it for some time, before claiming the obvious, "It is very old and faded."

"Unfortunately yes, but it is extremely important that we identify this man."

"There is something about the features of this officer. He was most definitely a naval officer, but his rank is difficult to make out, and yet his face appears familiar. I don't suppose this can be dated?"

"Unfortunately, not as far as I am aware except to say it is much older than fifteen years."

The Master then carefully placed the tinplate on top of his desk, before standing and stepping across to the door.

"Bear with me for a moment Inspector," he begged, before disappearing from the room.

Within a couple of minutes, Gardiner returned in the company of an elderly seafarer with a mop of grey hair, and a full beard hiding half his face. The man's features confirmed many years had been spent visiting the oceans of the world.

The Master introduced his rating as Michael Tomkins, the longest serving member in Her Majesty's Navy.

The old man gave a seaman's salute to the Inspector, before asking where the tinplate was.

Gardiner handed it to him, and again better use of the tallow candle was deployed. He stood on his bandy legs, scrutinising the faint portrait, and shaking his head, confessed, "It certainly looks familiar sir, but I can't quite put my finger on it. From the shape of the hat, I would say the man worked on the wooden ships, rather than the iron vessels we have today."

"Take your time, Mr. Tomkins, this is extremely important to the Inspector."

Then the veteran suddenly looked up at the Master, his watery eyes filled with optimism.

"The Victory," he loudly announced, "I know now where I have seen him, or his twin; in a painting of the surviving crew at Trafalgar. He served under His Lordship, Admiral Nelson in HMS Victory. Well I'll be blown down in a gale."

"By All the Saints, I think you are right Mr. Tomkins," the Master agreed, offering support to the old seaman's claim, "The same painting you refer to is at Chatham."

Turning to Rayner, Elias Gardiner explained that they would have to visit what was a principle naval dockyard, where ships were built and residential quarters for officers were located. They could make further enquiries at the small Maritime Museum in the same complex, and where the painting of the Victory's crew was kept.

Richard Rayner then asked if there was a crew listing for the Victory at the time of Trafalgar, confirming that the battle itself was fought some seventy years previously, in October of 1805. His mathematical mind calculated that, if what was being assumed was correct, and the officer in the tinplate was indeed a relative of the murdered sisters, then it was possible it could have been their father, Bartholomew Barratt.

"Yes, that will also be kept with other important historical documents at Chatham, but I shall have to accompany you Inspector, otherwise you will not be allowed access."

The following morning the two men set out early, travelling in an official Royal Navy carriage, and the man from Scotland Yard was extremely appreciative of the voluntary assistance being given to him by the Master at Arms. During the journey, the detective found his interest in shipbuilding and naval warfare was becoming more stimulated, as he listened to a specialist explaining various aspects entwined in the navy's history, right up to the present. He found Elias Gardiner to be more than just an amicable travelling companion, but one who displayed both dynamism and a vast knowledge of the subject upon which he had spent his virtual life studying.

It was mid-afternoon by the time the travellers from Portsmouth reached the Dockyard and Richard Rayner could not help but be impressed by the regimental layout of the institution. This was indeed the very heart of Britain's ability to effectively wager war on the open seas, and where the majority of the older wooden ships had been built throughout the centuries.

Gardiner pointed out that it was at Chatham where HMS Victory was built back in the middle of the last century. He also indicated two iron ships that were being fitted in dry dock, as their carriage headed across the historical site towards where the private museum was situated. Rayner was appreciative that the complex he was visiting wasn't accessible to the public in general.

When they finally arrived outside the front of the museum, they were greeted by a junior ranking officer, who immediately instructed a rating to stable the horses and clean the carriage. But before going further, the Master at Arms led the Inspector into a small enclosed refreshment area, situated on the end of a row of terraced properties used to accommodate naval officers and their families. There, both men were provided with light meals, and Gardiner participated in a measure of Pussers Rum, recommending the warming alcohol to Rayner. Not wanting to snub his host, the detective also drank the same spirit that was the official daily serving to men at sea.

The Inspector compared the drink favourably to a good brandy and told the Master so, who smiled appreciatively before leading the way back down a footpath, until they finally returned to their destination.

There was no official sign indicating the purpose of the brick-built building, and after climbing a set of concrete steps and passing through a set of double wooden doors, Rayner found himself standing in a square hallway with a black and white tiled floor. Elias Gardiner continued to lead the way up a wide-open staircase. There were a number of white marble busts of various former Admirals, including one of the most famous sailors in history, Horatio Nelson, which was perched on a tall plinth near the top of the stairs.

Although the building appeared to be void of other human beings, Rayner sensed a kind of cleanliness and organised environment that could only be synonymous with the military, or of course, the Royal Navy.

Having reached the landing on the second floor, from which the visitors could look down at the hallway below, the Master continued until they reached a closed door near to the end. When they entered, they stood on yet another highly polished tiled floor, and the detective was introduced to a small, wiry man, who they found seated at a small desk near to one of a number of large unobstructed windows.

The Guardian of the Museum stood to salute both visitors and Elias Gardiner explained the duties of the retired Boson. It was vitally important that the many historical exhibits which included true records of naval achievements, were constantly cared for and maintained. Then he turned to face one of the walls, illumined by natural light coming from yet another nearby window, and confirmed, "This is what we have come to see Inspector."

The large painting in oils was of a group of men standing and crouching on a quayside, with HMS Victory in the background. It was obviously an artist's record of the famous ship's crew, and the heading on the frame, below the painting itself read 'The survivors of HMS Victory after Trafalgar'.

The Master at Arms pointed to a man wearing an officer's uniform who was standing in the back row.

"What do you think, sir?"

Richard Rayner was amazed and stood back, gazing at virtually the same face that appeared in the tinplate. In fact, he held the portrait he had brought with him from London, up next to the man in the painting and smiled to himself. The old seafarer, Michael Tomkins, had been fairly accurate when he had said it was a replica of the man in the tinplate.

"I am perplexed," he remarked to the Master, "This has to be the same officer. Have we that list of the crew I mentioned before?"

The Master turned to the Guardian, and enquired where the Victory's crew list was kept.

"Just over this way sir," the wiry man with a pair of rimless spectacles perched on the end of his nose, confirmed, "Follow me."

He led them across the room to a far corner where there was a glass cabinet supported by a wooden stand.

Again, Rayner was impressed by the way the smaller man placed a pair of white linen gloves on each hand, before unlocking the cabinet with a small key. Then he took the small pages of parchment from the enclosure and carefully carried them to his desk by the window. Having placed them down, he then invited both visitors to look at them, with a strict condition that none of the parchments were to be touched by any human hand.

"Please tell me gentlemen when you require me to turn a page over," he requested.

The first page on view was that of the ship's ratings, and Rayner asked if the guardian could turn to the list of surviving officers. When that appeared, he scrutinised each name, until he came to the one nominal he was hoping to find. 'Jnr. Lieutenant B. Barratt'.

Turning to the small custodian, the Inspector then asked, "Do we know during which years these particular men served on the Victory?"

"Only that this list was compiled following the Battle of Trafalgar and was delivered to us in 1807, two years after that campaign. The Victory herself was launched from here as early as 1765, and wasn't paid off until 1825. Ever since then, she has remained at Portsmouth in dry dock, as the flagship of the Navy's Commander-in-Chief, but of course, most of the crew who served in her at Trafalgar have long gone."

The Inspector considered asking to see if any duty record of Lieutenant Barratt was available to inspect, but then realised there was no need, as Henry Bustle had already confirmed the same man had trained and worked as a Cabinet Maker in Coventry, before leaving for London.

He thanked the two naval personnel for their help and assistance, and was invited to stay at the dockyard over night, but declined offering his apologies. Richard Rayner's return to Scotland Yard, had now become a matter of the utmost urgency.

Chapter Thirteen

The news that Scotland Yard had re-opened the case into the murders of the two sisters in Whitechapel, eventually filtered across to the Continent. When a local baker who supplied a small French village mentioned the story to one of the local inhabitants, the recipient showed a great deal of interest. There had also been a newspaper report of a statement made by a Superintendent Morgan, linking a more recent murder to the same Inquiry, which caused the same man to smile inwardly.

It was mid-afternoon when he continued his daily stroll through the vineyard adjacent to his Chateau, sensing the musty smell that was lingering in the warm air. As he progressed on his walk, he remained confident the English Police would bungle this latest attempt to find him, in the same way as they had done so previously. He stopped to pick a grape, before tasting its sharpness; too much for his liking and deciding another week or two was required before harvesting. As he stood there amongst the vines, memories began to flood back, beyond that fifteen-year period to a time when his wife was still alive. The emotions he was feeling began to strike home and he wiped a small tear from his eye, reminding himself to revisit the grave soon. Not knowing whether the sensations he was feeling were a result of having lost his wife in such a brutal way. Or could it be because once again, he had become a hunted man?

Henry Bustle was late arriving in his Detective Inspector's office at Scotland Yard, which was an event as rare as the many Christian Charities in the capital, serving up roast beef to the needy. And yet, the Sergeant had been guilty of such a sin twice now in the space of a week.

Richard Rayner made no comment, suspecting that his Sergeant's lapse had in all probability been the result of his fitness levels not having yet returned to normal. However, his colleague offered his most profuse apologies, as soon as he entered the room.

"How did it go with your man in prison?" the Inspector enquired with genuine interest.

Bustle told him of the accusations made by Royston Whittle, and brief details of the information his man had provided regarding the Brick Lane Ratters gang. He made specific mention of their supposed leader, Black Jake Quarry.

At first, Rayner felt some disdain and his eyes reflected a great deal of doubt.

"Do you give any credence to Mr. Whittle's information Henry?"

"At first I didn't Inspector, but then again, he has never dealt me a bad card before and there was no reason why he should lie to me on this occasion. What he told me, was feasible. The murders were motiveless, and according to Whittle's account, the reason was connected with some kind of distasteful initiation new recruits to the gang had to go through to prove themselves."

"Do we know where this fellow, Black Jake can be found now?" Rayner asked, still appearing dubious.

"According to one of my old snitches in Whitechapel, I called on before arriving here, our man works as a porter at the London Hospital."

"Well, he is certainly local to the area of the murders, and it seems is still prominent in the district. Did we get the name of the so-called recruit your man mentioned?"

"No, he didn't know it and at least I believed that part of his story."

"I'm not sure whether we should believe any of the story he has shared with us Henry."

"There's only one way to find out," the Sergeant suggested.

The thoroughfares were still hazardous, although passable by that time, and as the two detectives journeyed back towards Whitechapel, Richard Rayner explained what he had discovered in Portsmouth during his recent visit.

"So, the naval connection to the sisters' murders continues," the Sergeant remarked.

"Yes it does seem that way Henry, and unless we obtain evidence to show that Black Jake Quarry is our man, our next move must be to obtain even more detailed information about the victims' family background."

When they arrived outside the front gates of the London Hospital, Rayner paid the cabbie, before both men cautiously made their way along the slippery driveway, until reaching the front doors. Once inside they found the reception area as busy as Smithfield Market on a day in the middle of the week. There were a host of individuals cluttering up the confined area; some with open wounds on display, others sitting pale faced on wooden chairs, waiting to receive medical attention. There were even those with various ailments visible, lying prostrate on top of the tiled floor.

Rayner managed to stop a nursing sister who appeared extremely harassed, having to organise those who had yet to be attended to.

"I'm sorry sister," he said, "Just a second or two of your time, if I may." He introduced himself to the lady, before enquiring whether she knew of a porter working there by the name of Jake Quarry.

The sister shook her head and suggested that the Inspector sought out Alfred Davis, the Head Porter, who she described as a man who would be wearing a brown cow gown with blonde hair. She directed them towards the back of the building, where she thought Mr. Davis might be working.

Rayner tipped his hat to the nursing official in appreciation, before releasing her.

The two detectives then began their search amongst the bedlam that seemed to be occupying every part of the hospital they visited in search of the Head Porter. Having been directed by various people to a number of different sections of the hospital, finally they found their man supervising the delivery of a load of non-descript boxes off an open cart, outside the rear of the premises.

"Mr. Alfred Davis?" the Inspector enquired of the man.

"That's me, who wants to know?" the man said, turning to face the inquisitor.

Rayner told him, and then asked if he had a Jake Quarry working for him as a porter.

"Big Jake, of course, you'll find him on the first floor Inspector. He's on the carnage run today."

"The carnage run?"

"Sorry," the man apologised, "He's wheeling patients between wards and the theatre for surgery. We just call it that because there's always carnage takes place, once a poor soul is handed over to the surgeons."

Rayner smiled and then asked, "How good a worker is Mr. Quarry?"

"He does his turn right enough, but tends to get aggressive when you topple his apple cart. Does this mean I shall have to be looking for a new porter to take his place?"

"Not necessarily."

Alfred Davis then turned to the man unloading the cardboard boxes and told him to take a break, and he would return shortly. He then led the way back inside the hospital, with both detectives following him.

"I wouldn't work in this place for double the wages they pay me at the Yard," the Sergeant whispered to his Inspector, as they made their way up a flight of stairs to the first floor.

"Oh, I'm not so sure, Henry. It doesn't seem much different from a rowdy public house on a Saturday night," Rayner answered, jokingly.

Jake Quarry was a colossus of a man, with shoulder length black hair and a heavy gold ear ring protruding from a lobe. His face showed signs of having led a violent life, mapped with various scars and a bulbous, disjointed nose that must have been broken on many occasions. His large mouth was grinning, as the supervisor and two visitors approached him.

The Head Porter introduced Rayner and Bustle to the man, who was grasping one end of a trolley, obviously heading back to a ward to collect yet another patient requiring the attention of the surgeons' knives.

"They just want a few words with you, Jake," Davis explained.

"We are making enquiries into an incident that took place fifteen years ago, in Mount Street," the Inspector announced, "And would like to ask you a few questions about any knowledge you might have about that."

The big man looked startled and grimaced.

"What kind of questions?" he grunted.

"I think it would be better if you came with us to Scotland Yard, and we can sort it all out there."

Quarry looked directly at the Head Porter, who had stood back a couple of places, and then confirmed in a loud, gruff voice, "I ain't going anywhere with you. I have more work to do here."

"That's okay my friend, I'm sure Mr. Davis here can manage without you for a short time," Rayner said, in a quiet and calm voice, steeling himself for the inevitable.

"I ain't coming with you, so you can ask your questions here and now."

The porter's aggressive attitude, referred to earlier by the Head Porter, was now being directed towards the detectives. Rayner decided the only way their man was going to leave the hospital premises with them, was if he was carried out. But he made one more effort to subdue Quarry, and remained calmly quiet.

"You are being treated as a possible witness at the moment Jake, so we really do need your co-operation."

"Fuck off. I know how you jaspers work, and I ain't coming with you, and that's final."

Quarry then began to push the trolley through them and Henry Bustle immediately grabbed the porter by an arm, feeling the solid muscle of the man's bicep.

The porter tried to yank himself away from the Sergeant's grip, but failed. So, in retaliation, he screamed out once again his objections to being manhandled and unleashed a vicious punch towards Bustle's head, which the detective managed to duck. There was only one direction in which the men from Scotland Yard could now go, and Richard Rayner grabbed the man's other arm, before their prisoner kicked out, sending the trolley racing down the corridor. The last thing the Inspector needed at that moment was a running battle with such a hostile human body builder, but there was no other option.

Quarry was strong and unfortunately for the officers, was prepared to fight. Swinging the arm which Rayner was grasping, he forced the Inspector to release his grip, causing him to be flung through the air like a rag doll, until being slammed against a wall.

Henry Bustle reacted immediately and put everything behind a punch to the porter's mid-drift, but that had no effect and Quarry just grinned at him before unloading one of his own closed fists. The heavy blow hit the Sergeant in the side of the face, sending him reeling down to the tiled floor. The unco-operative man then took off, in an attempt to escape the detectives' clutches.

Rayner was still trying to regain his breath but managed to regain his feet. Like a Mercurial messenger, he raced after the fugitive before diving forward and hitting the man around his knees. Both men fell to the floor and the Inspector managed to get on top of the suspect, before pummeling him with a torrent of punches to his face. Finally, the fight within Quarry disappeared, and the man just lay there, subdued, with his face covered in blood, as were the aching knuckles of both Rayner's fists.

Bustle quickly joined the Inspector and both men turned their prisoner on to his stomach, before the Sergeant clapped a pair of heavy handcuffs around the captured man's wrists. Only then did the pair feel confident they had finally captured their man.

"Just a few questions, Inspector?" the Head Porter sarcastically quipped, before all three made their way towards the stairs, with both detectives still gasping for breath, and the side of Henry Bustle's face beginning to swell up again. Thankfully the prisoner's appearance confirmed he had lost the battle.

For added security, once they were back at Scotland Yard, Richard Rayner insisted that Jake Quarry was shackled further with leg irons, before being placed in an interview room. Once satisfied the man had been sufficiently secured and ready to be questioned without offering more violence, the interview commenced. Both the Inspector and Sergeant sat opposite the prisoner with a constable standing near to the door, just in case.

"We understand Jake that you used to be the leader of a small band of rag and muffins known as the Brick Lane Ratters, is that correct?"

The prisoner's hands were still cuffed behind his back, making it awkward for him to sit comfortably, a condition which Rayner was happy to allow to continue. He looked down at the floor; his face looking a sorrowful mess as a result of the Inspector's vicious and prolonged attack.

"They weren't rag and muffins," Quarry answered, defiantly.

"And in those days, you were known as Black Jake, is that right?"

The man's eyes lifted to stare directly at Rayner, before he answered tenaciously, "Fuck off. You bastards are only interested in locking me up so just get on with it."

"It seems to me that, considering the reputation your gang of hard men had in those days, I should have thought it a little demeaning to murder two helpless old women."

Black Jake's eyes widened, but he showed no other reaction, other than one of surprise.

"I ain't murdered any old ladies," He paused and exhaled deeply, before continuing, "What's this all about? You lobsters come to my place of work and attack me, and then accuse me of all sorts of things which I ain't had anything to do with."

"No, you are wrong Jake. We are only accusing you of murdering two helpless women, and I also believe, the atrocities were part of some ritual you and your gang of miscreants participated in, when assessing the worthiness of a new recruit, and that's what we want to know my friend; the name of the man who went into that Tripe Shop with you."

The prisoner just stared at the Inspector, and shook his head.

"Mister, I ain't got a clue what you're going on about."

"Very well, Jake, we shall just have to leave you to the hangman. Of course it could be in your interest, and would probably save your life, if you would be more co-operative, especially if it wasn't you who killed the old women, but the man who was with you. But if you want to be bravado and protect the real killer, then that is a matter for yourself."

"I still don't know what you're talking about." He stopped talking, as both Rayner and Bustle stood from their chairs and stepped across the room towards where the constable was guarding the door.

"Look," Quarry continued in a less aggressive voice, "We was just a bunch of kids in those days, looking for some fun, and that's all. I've no idea where you've got this story from that we murdered two old women in a shop, but it just ain't true. The most we ever did was batter members of some other street gang, and nick a few bits of fruit from the market."

"That's not good enough, Jake. We are not fools and have empirical evidence to charge you with both murders. You are about to shake hands with the hangman, my friend," Rayner explained persuasively, before leaving the interview room with Henry Bustle behind him.

When they reached the Inspector's office, the first question the Sergeant asked was, "Do you believe him?"

"Yes, I do Henry," Rayner answered, "There is something about his character and behaviour that makes me believe, he would have been too egotistic to commit the atrocities we are investigating. What about you?"

Bustle shook his head and confessed, "I'm not sure. I hear what you are saying, but fifteen years ago who knows what grotesque criminal acts he could have got up to. The man's a bloody animal."

"Well, if what your informant has told us, there was another man involved, and that being the case, and having already planted the seed in our man's head, let's wait and see if he decides to give us his name. Only a fool facing the rope would decline to take such an opportunity to save his own skin."

"I'll give him a few minutes to think about it, and go back and see if he's had a change of heart."

"What you need to do Henry is get some ice on the side of your face, before your handsome looks deteriorate further."

Chapter Fourteen

Superintendent Morgan was sitting quietly behind his desk when Richard Rayner appeared in response to the summons he had received to attend forthwith.

"You sent for me sir."

Morgan looked up from the file of papers he had been scrutinising and thanked the Inspector for attending so quickly. There was a veiled hostility in the Superintendent's manner, and an ingratiating smile that was more realistically, a smirk of malice and easily detectable.

Morgan appeared calm on the surface, when he asked his Inspector if there had been any progress in the Barratt sisters' Inquiry, and Rayner briefly explained the course of action taken earlier that day in relation to the arrest of Jake Quarry.

"Are you convinced this is the killer we have been looking for?" the Superintendent quietly asked.

"No sir, I have grave doubts, although if he was more co-operative I feel confident Quarry could provide us with useful information, but it does appear his mind is influenced by the Whitechapel villains' code of non-complicity."

The volcano was beginning to rumble, as a prelude to a full eruption.

"Then, if you have 'grave doubts' about this man's involvement in the murders, why in Hell's name are you wasting time talking to the man down in the cells?"

"Because it was a line of enquiry we could not ignore, and the information had come from a proven and credible informant, sir."

"A convict who would say anything in return for a packet of baccy."

"That is your opinion sir."

It was then that Frederick Morgan's character changed from a subdued, enquiring senior officer, to one of a grizzled veteran who had become extremely disillusioned by the absence of any positive result.

"I'm beginning to believe Inspector that your tailor's dummy methods are not sufficiently adequate to bring about a satisfactory conclusion to this case."

"Again, you are entitled to your opinion sir." Rayner was stung by the criticism, especially the inference to his personal choice of clothing, but remained calm and tenacious.

"I've always believed the reputation you seem to have self-initiated, is one that is exaggerated and over rated. You have spent weeks now, posturing and running about like a headless chicken sir, and to date, you have failed to give us anything remotely positive. We still remain in the dark without any idea of who the killer of those two old ladies happens to be." Morgan could not hide his increasing anger and frustration, giving the impression that he had been hewn from the same rock as a tormented animal caught in a trap.

"I disagree," Rayner retorted, in his own defence, "As you are aware sir, during the initial stages of any complex inquiry such as this, there is a need to eliminate certain suspects and lines of inquiry, but I am confident that the more we probe, the closer we are getting to the real killer. I also believe the Commissioner would concur."

The Superintendent leapt from his seat, with his face darkening by the second, and loudly protested, "I will not be hoodwinked mister, in the same way as you appear to have falsely convinced the Commissioner of your fictitious abilities."

Now, Rayner was beginning to feel anger, which was a rarity for the Detective Inspector. He glared back at Morgan, and allowed a few seconds to pass by whilst composing himself. Then for the first time in his career, the Yard's top detective turned his senior officer's legs into jelly, by making his immediate decision known.

"In the circumstances then Superintendent, and considering your lowly opinion of my abilities, I am compelled to resign my current position with immediate effect. I shall submit the appropriate report within the next few minutes. Would you be so kind as to find me another posting, where I can continue working during the time I require to review my position in the force." Rayner then turned and left the office, slamming the door behind him. With all the jibing and frequent criticizing, never before had Morgan managed to rile him as much as he'd done so on this occasion.

Frederick Morgan just stood at his desk stunned. The side of the Detective Inspector's character he'd just witnessed was new to him. He realised he had wounded the man deeply. His body felt limp and he gasped for air, as he fell back into his chair. If he had given any thought to his words prior to that short meeting, he would never have guessed they would have resulted in such drastic action being taken by Richard Rayner. The problem the Superintendent was now facing was his knowledge that his Inspector did not lie, or exaggerate; Richard Rayner would be fully committed towards going through with what was more than a mere threat. He also knew deep down, that although he was inclined to vent his frustration, at times unfairly on Rayner, the Inspector was the most successful and hardest working officer in the Detective Department. In addition to those facts, Morgan was also aware that the loss to his department would be immense, and he himself would be the subject of some vitriolic criticism from the Commissioner, Sir Edmund Henderson.

When Richard Rayner entered his own office, the anger he had been feeling beforehand had somewhat dissipated, and he was a lot calmer and objective. Ignoring Henry Bustle, who was sitting at the side of his Inspector's desk, ploughing his way through the dossier of papers they had compiled since the beginning of the Case Review, the Inspector sat down and began to handwrite his report.

"Anything I can help you with Inspector?" the Sergeant asked, noticing the despondent look on Rayner's face.

The Inspector stopped writing and sat back in his chair, before quietly explaining to Bustle that he had just resigned his position within the Detective Branch.

At first, the Sergeant's eyes were blank. He was totally shocked and stood from his seat.

"Why in God's name have you done that?"

"To succeed in any investigation of this type Henry, we cannot achieve success without the full support of our senior officers, and I am afraid Superintendent Morgan has lost his faith in my abilities, leaving me with no other choice."

"Is the man mad? Everybody knows there is no other detective working in this building who is capable of achieving what you have done. This is insane, and how in the Lord's name are we going to conclude this Inquiry without you?"

"That is very good of you to say Henry, and I thank you for your kind salutations, but as I have already explained, I have been left marooned with no other option."

What small snippets of information were reported in the French newspapers did not escape the man's attention, and it had become a daily habit to read through every page. The village near where he lived was quiet, and apart from a baker's shop and a small schoolhouse, the remaining buildings were mostly cottages in which local farmers and farm workers lived.

Although confident that the British Police would never get close to identifying him, there was still a nagging doubt in the back of his mind, having read complimentary reports about the Scotland Yard detective who was leading the hunt for the killer. It appeared that this Detective Inspector Richard Rayner was the only threat to him. Could it be possible that the officer could eventually find a path open through which he could track the Frenchman down? The killer of the Barratt sisters' needed a contingency plan, just in case.

The sun was at its zenith, as he sat on the patio at the back of his Chateau, tasting his own red wine and exercising his mind on various considerations he should make, if he felt he was being drawn closer to any risk of being detained. He was not the kind of man to sit back and wait until things happened that could be to his detriment. He was quite prepared to make things happen, if that was the course of action required. But what could he do should the Scotland Yard detective suddenly appear at his front door? Then he accepted he was becoming paranoid about matters that had not yet taken place, and the reality of his situation was that he would remain safe and concealed, provided he remained calm and deliberate.

He finally decided to do nothing but continue to monitor what was happening in London. After all, this Inspector Rayner was only one man, and contrary to his reputation being reported in the newspapers, would not be capable of performing miracles.

"It is Inspector Rayner's decision sir," the Superintendent insisted, as he groveled before the Commissioner's desk, "I failed to get the officer to change his mind."

"I am not a complete fool, Frederick," Sir Edmund answered, "You have baited Rayner, of that I have no doubt."

"I cannot support a man who is unhappy working in the Detective Department sir."

"Then let me be crystal clear Superintendent. Richard Rayner is not only an exceptional detective; he is the best investigator we have at Scotland Yard by a country mile. Nod your head man, because failure to agree with me is very likely to put your own position in jeopardy."

Morgan nodded profusely.

"So, I will not accept this resignation from Rayner, do you understand me?"

"Yes sir." In fairness to Morgan, although having been admonished by the Commissioner, he was delighted that the Head of the Metropolitan Police was actually blocking Rayner's exit from his department. The Superintendent had always viewed the Inspector with the utmost respect and admiration, and was aware of his own man management failings, although he would never openly admit the same. It was now all about, Frederick Morgan saving face.

"You will go directly back to Mr. Rayner and persuade him to remain in the Detective Department, even if to do so would mean you sir, washing his dirty linen and front doorstep for a week or more. Under no circumstances will that man leave us, is that clear?"

"Yes sir."

"Then come back to me with the news that Richard Rayner has had a change of heart. When I make mention of your own position,

Superintendent, I speak in earnest."

"Yes sir. I fully understand. Leave it to me."

"Grovel man, if you need to, and put an immediate end to this hostility that appears to exist between you both."

Richard Rayner could not remember the last occasion he had actually taken leave from work, and was already planning to take a voyage in order to allow himself time to review his situation. He could not possibly envisage returning to uniform and patrolling the streets, following the adventures and excitement he had experienced as a Detective Inspector, in particular the successes he had achieved. Rayner was convinced that once he had given sufficient thought to his future, he would leave the Metropolitan Police altogether, but that holiday voyage would be important. Perhaps a return to lecturing would be agreeable, although he was doubtful. But for now, the South of France appealed to him. There was always the possibility of meeting the girl of his dreams, getting married and raising a family. It had always been his intention to do that in any case, eventually.

A glum and bewildered, Henry Bustle had left his Inspector's office, to revisit Jake Quarry downstairs, leaving Rayner alone to collect his personal things, before he would leave the building to take the leave owing to him. Of course, he would not absence himself until he had said a final farewell to his old trusted friend, and was feeling melancholy, as he continued to empty his desk and pack his case.

Frederick Morgan had not obtained the rank of Superintendent without first displaying his ability to deal with critical situations. Richard Rayner was not the only outstanding linguist working at Scotland Yard, but the senior detective knew he would have to call on every skill at his disposal if he was to accede to the Commissioner's request.

As he entered the Inspector's office through an open door, the self-acclaimed highly skilled negotiator, began to build the bridge he was desperate to complete, by approaching his task with complimentary submissions.

"Well Richard, I must confess I will miss you. I am now in a quandary how we are going to replace our greatest detective. As much as I have toiled in attempting to identify a suitable replacement, I cannot."

Richard Rayner turned to face the Superintendent, finding it difficult to come to terms with such a drastic change of attitude now being voiced by the man who earlier had thrust a dagger through his heart, with a volley of personal insults. He nodded and smiled in his usual confident manner.

"Before you leave us Richard, perhaps you could tell me what course of action you were contemplating in the Barratt Inquiry?"

"Of course Superintendent," Rayner willingly confirmed, "I strongly feel that the answer lies somewhere in the sisters' past and that there is a vital link in their background."

"You suspect a relative of the ladies then?"

"That could be the case, but I do suspect the killer might well have been linked to a distant relative, but there are two phases you will need to visit. It is imperative that we reveal every aspect of the victims' past history, including each individual related to them in some way, and secondly, we need to concentrate on a naval influence being present when trying to identify that family link."

The two men were now having the kind of conversation that should have taken priority on the last time they had met. Hostility and personal insults from Superintendent Morgan had been responsible for, what could only be described as a regretful divorce between the participants.

Morgan took a seat, before producing a cigar and lighting the same. He then diffidently asked, "Who would you recommend is sufficiently suitable to make such complex enquiries then Richard?" The man had a plan of entrapment and was working towards it with all the precision he could practice.

On seeing the Superintendent crouched in a chair, Rayner also stepped around his desk and sat down, before answering, "Sergeant Bustle must be retained on the Inquiry, as he knows as much as I do about the investigations we have made thus far. As for a replacement being identified for myself, I could never be so arrogant as to suggest another officer."

"What you mean is that you could not identify anyone else who possesses the same qualities as yourself? And I would agree with you. So why can you not continue with the Inquiry yourself Richard?"

Rayner sat there, just looking across at the Superintendent who was now slowly disappearing behind clouds of smoke, which was not unusual.

Finally, he quietly answered, "Give me one good reason why I should not leave and enjoy a break in the South of France sir."

"I can give you several man. In my opinion, this particular Case Review can only be brought to a successful conclusion if you continued with the investigation. Also Richard, I offer my sincerest apologies for the insulting remarks I made to you earlier."

Richard Rayner never believed that he would ever hear such words come out of Frederick Morgan's mouth, and was genuinely surprised.

"Then Superintendent, I accept your apology, which leaves me with no other option but to continue in my present position."

"Thank you," a relieved Morgan gasped, standing and stepping across the room, before offering the Inspector his hand in friendship, which was taken willingly.

"I have erred on this occasion, and I have apologised," the Superintendent confessed, "But I will say this Inspector, it will be the only time such an event will occur."

"I accept that Superintendent, and in return you have my word I shall bring this killer to you, no matter what it takes."

Chapter Fifteen

Coventry was a pleasant city with broad cobbled streets and tall spires. It immediately reminded Richard Rayner of another favourite city of his, where he had spent a great deal of his student days studying and lecturing in Mathematics. Oxford's history and magnificent architectural buildings had been like a magnet to him, and although a location such as the one he was now visiting was on a much smaller scale, it brought to mind memories of those past halcyon days. But Coventry possessed no seats of learning or academic institutions, in which the highest standard of research and study had been achieved. Instead, the city boasted numerous factories attached to the outlets of specialised and highly skilled watch and clock makers, with a sprinkling of sewing machine and bicycle manufacturers.

Having left the train which had brought him up from London, the Inspector first approached the Station Master, a grey haired man with white hair protruding from beneath his uniform hat, and a bushy moustache to match. The man must have been in his early sixties, heading towards his retirement day, and looked extremely smart with black shoes that glistened in the daylight. He had a jovial face and blew his whistle to signal the train that had carried Richard Rayner, to continue on the remainder of its journey north, before turning to answer the detective's question.

"A Cabinet Maker by the name of Barratt you say?"

"Yes, but I am going back probably a matter of some forty years or more."

"Good grief, do I really look that old," the Station Master joked, chuckling to himself, "Well, I've lived here all of my life and would have been in my early twenties about that time, but cannot I'm afraid, personally recollect such a family. In those days the majority of traders were the same as they are today, mostly watch makers, although they're slowly disappearing now under pressure brought about by the Swiss manufacturers."

"I'm not sure how long Bartholomew Barratt would have lived in Coventry, I can only estimate it would have been about twenty or thirty years. He was at Trafalgar with Lord Nelson, if that's any help."

The mention of the famous sea battle seemed to rouse the Station Master and Rayner noticed a glint come to his watery eyes.

"I seem to remember a man living close by in Hay Lane, who everybody revered as a result of the part he'd played on HMS Victory. I recall he was some kind of a hero, or so people around here thought at the time."

The Railway employee then turned and called to an elderly porter who was busy working at the opposite end of the platform upon which they were standing. The man was tidying one of a number of flower-boxes, which added some natural colour to the station, making the surroundings more pleasant on the eye of the paying travellers.

"A word if you please, Samuel," the Station Master solicited.

The porter carried his broom, as he walked the distance of the platform, before reaching the couple.

His supervisor reiterated the enquiry being made by the Inspector, hoping that perhaps the man dressed in a black waistcoat beneath a well-worn company issued jacket, might remember something useful.

Without hesitation, the porter recognised the name of the man who had been on the Victory at Trafalgar.

"Barratt the Cabinet Maker, yes, he had a shop in Hay Lane which is now owned by old Julius Feather, the watchmaker. I remember I was only a lad at the time, and people were always paying homage to him as a result of his naval experiences. The man was most certainly a hero in those days and I think if he robbed the local squire, he would have been allowed to get away with it."

"You say that it's now a watchmaker's shop?"

"Oh yes, has been for some years. I would imagine Mr. Barratt is long gone by now."

"Do you recall two daughters the Cabinet Maker had at the time?"

"No sir, but that doesn't mean to say there weren't any."

"Could you direct me please, to Hay Lane?"

"Of course," the Station Master agreed, looking at his pocket watch and noting the next train wasn't due for twenty minutes. He then explained that the address was within walking distance and told the man from London the quickest route.

Richard Rayner thanked both men for their assistance and began his trek from the Railway Station, heading away from the city centre.

When he finally arrived in Hay Lane, it didn't take the Inspector long to find the small shop he sought, which had a bowed ground floor window and the name of Julius Feather, Watch and Clock Maker, over the doorway.

Meanwhile, Henry Bustle, having interviewed Jake Quarry once again without having any joy, decided to begin the tasks set him by Rayner. Inwardly, he was seething at the realisation that his convict informant, Royston Whittle, had led him and Richard Rayner a merry dance. It was a debt he now owed the incarcerated man, and vowed to repay him in full at a later, more convenient time.

Throughout the remainder of that day, the Sergeant attempted to obtain as much information as he possibly could, visiting various record offices and parish churches. By the time the light was fading his legs ached and the soles on his boots were a lot thinner than they had been when he'd first put them on his feet that morning. However, he was slowly beginning to build up a clearer picture of the two sisters' backgrounds, and more useful information was forthcoming when he visited the Admiralty near Marble Arch.

Bustle found the Royal Navy to be an amicable ally, who opened their records to him quite willingly. By the time he stepped from the large white building, he was satisfied that he had accomplished a great deal of success, and couldn't wait to share his findings with Richard Rayner, once his Inspector returned from Coventry.

Julius Feather was a wizened old man with a hump across the back of one shoulder, which almost doubled him up.

Rayner found him crouching over a small mechanism at the back of the shop, and had to wait a little while for the old man to step up to the small counter.

"And what can I do for you young man?" the watchmaker asked, in a crackling and high-pitched voice.

The Inspector introduced himself, and explained that he was making enquiries into a serious double murder that had taken place some fifteen years previously. He then enquired whether Julius Feather had actually purchased the shop premises directly from Bartholomew Barratt, the Cabinet Maker.

"Heavens no lad," the watchmaker confirmed, "My father did that, when he was alive that is. He bought it from the hero of Trafalgar and his wife, long before he passed on and left it to me, not that it's ever been worth much more than a couple of farthings, and a lot of back breaking hard work."

"Do you remember Mr. Barratt and his wife? They had two daughters I believe, Gertrude and Emily."

"Of course I do. I was still learning the trade in those days and came here with my Papa, God rest his soul, when he was negotiating the purchase."

"Pray tell me, what were they like, can you recall?"

"They all worshipped the man from around here, because he had served under Vice-Admiral Nelson and had fought at Trafalgar. I recall it was obvious to us that he didn't really want to leave here, but he did, alas."

"Why do you seem so sad when you say that Mr. Feather?"

"Oh, I'm being silly lad. It's because, being so popular, there was no real reason why he should sell out, but I do remember he told us his wife was very ill, and he thought he could access better doctors for her in London."

"What kind of a man was he, in your opinion?"

"Well now, as I've said, I was a young man then, still learning the trade from my father but from what little I can recollect, Mr. Barratt was a kind enough and stable gentleman, who was obviously totally committed to his wife and daughters."

Rayner placed both elbows on top of the counter and spoke with a quieter voice, when he asked, "Do you recollect whether there was any other reason Mr. Barratt left for London?"

The old man shook his head, and answered, "No, it was like I said, his wife was very ill. In fact, I seem to recall she passed on before the family actually made the move. She died from the Consumption I believe. Anyway, they left amongst a great deal of sympathy from the locals."

"So, Mrs. Barratt is buried here in Coventry?"

"Oh yes, she most certainly is. I think her grave is up the hill in the

Cathedral graveyard. Are you sure you wouldn't like me to take a look at your watch sir?"

"No, but thank you. You have been a great help. Could you tell me if Mrs. Barratt's grave is marked?"

"I believe so."

Before leaving, Rayner placed a two-shilling piece in the old man's hand, which immediately brought a look of great appreciation on to Julius Feather's face. The Inspector's next and probably final visit would be to Bartholomew Barratt's wife's grave.

Coventry's Cathedral wasn't difficult to locate, as its magnificent steeple tower reached up high, and its fourteenth century Gothic structure looked down on the city, in similar fashion to a protective and caring guardian of the populace. The Inspector wondered how much the Barratt family would have been made to pay for the privilege of being allowed to hold a funeral and burial there.

By the time he had reached the impressive structure, his legs were becoming weary. It had been a long day and the events of the previous day involving the altercation with Frederick Morgan, were now beginning to take their toll on the Inspector.

Rayner was pleased that the number of graves in the Cathedral's grounds weren't that numerous, and within a short space of time he finally identified the headstone with the name of Elizabeth Barratt engraved upon it. Again, no expense had been spared, the marker having been manufactured from white marble, but what really attracted the Inspector's attention was that the headstone was so clean. In fact, both the marker and the grave itself appeared as if they had just been placed there. To maintain the location in such prime condition Rayner realised that it must have been visited frequently by someone who cared for the person occupying the ground beneath. There was a vase filled with fresh flowers at the foot of the headstone, which supported his suspicion that it was the subject of regular attendances.

He leant down to examine the small bouquet that had obviously been placed into the vase with the utmost care, and noticed a small piece of white card resting at the back of the floral display. On the card was a short-handwritten message, which read, 'RIP Elizabeth from your loving grandson, Herbert'.

Rayner straightened and tried to recall the handwriting found in the missive hidden inside the back of the painting of HMS Victoria, which once belonged to Gertrude Barratt. The Inspector was convinced the writing on both items had been written by the same hand, and left the graveyard after taking possession of the second message.

When he boarded his train to take him back to London, Rayner allowed himself a feeling of contentment. The net was closing quickly now, and he was more confident that the promise he had made to Superintendent Morgan, back at Scotland Yard, would soon be fulfilled. There was no doubting, Herbert Barratt's name was becoming more prominent on their list of suspects, yet it still wrangled with the Inspector that a man could have possibly murdered his own mother, and in such a violent and brutal manner. If of course, Herbert Barratt had been Gertrude's son.

Chapter Sixteen

Upon his return to Scotland Yard, Richard Rayner felt obliged not to leave Superintendent Morgan distanced from the Inquiry. He immediately updated his senior officer on the knowledge he had acquired during his visit to Coventry.

Much to his pleasant surprise, he found the man to be more communicative. Gone were the raging and frustrating episodes that had marred their relationship, and the Superintendent listened to Rayner's account intently. Morgan agreed that the journey had been worthwhile and that his Inspector had made some progress. Both men also agreed that the solution to the mystery lay somewhere in links to the victims' family ties.

When meeting with Henry Bustle, the top detective was impatient to hear what his Sergeant had unraveled in his efforts to obtain a more concise account of the Barratt's past history. He found his man waiting in his office, perusing through his notebook.

As he had done with Superintendent Morgan, Rayner updated his junior officer before comparing the handwriting on both the missive found concealed in the oil painting, and that recovered from Elizabeth Barratt's grave. There was little doubt, the two messages had been written by the same hand and that Gertrude's illegitimate son, Herbert, had been responsible for both.

Sergeant Bustle then produced a handwritten portrait of the stricken family's members, which he had compiled earlier. It clearly showed that the victims' grandfather, Jacob Barratt was born in 1748 and had been a naval rating who spent a great deal of his service with the Royal Navy, travelling the Indies.

"I could only go back as far as Jacob Barratt," Bustle explained, "And I suspect there must have been some wealth accrued by the family before his time, because he was able to pay for his son, Bartholomew, to attend the Royal Naval College at Dartmouth, before he was commissioned as an officer." Bustle was referring to the dead victims' father.

"I agree Henry," Rayner said, "It does seem unlikely that such expenses would have been met from a naval rating's pay."

"According to Admiralty records, Jacob's son was born in 1785 and later served on HMS Victory at the time of the Battle of Trafalgar, which was fought in 1805."

"Yes, he was a prominent figure in Coventry as a result of being a survivor from that action," the Inspector confirmed, sitting at his desk and making his own notes, as Bustle related the details to him.

"It does seem strange however that, Bartholomew Barratt left the service just a couple of years after Trafalgar, when he settled in Coventry."

"It might have been the result of the man having had his fill of navy life," Rayner suggested, "And felt the need to fulfil a desire to be a Cabinet Maker."

The Sergeant nodded, before continuing.

"Well, I also discovered from the Admiralty that, Bartholomew Barratt and his wife, Elizabeth, had a daughter, Emily, born in 1805 whilst he was still serving in the navy."

"That being the same year as Trafalgar."

"Yes, and their second daughter was born three years later, in 1808 which would have been Gertrude."

"And by that time, our man had already left the navy and was living in Coventry."

The Sergeant then went on to explain that between 1808 and 1830 there was no record of the family, until their names appeared in a parish register in Bermondsey. It confirmed that Bartholomew Barratt and his two daughters were by 1827 living in London.

"According to the watchmaker, Julius Feather, who I spoke with yesterday, Bartholomew's wife Elizabeth died before the family left for London," Rayner explained, "So it would appear that the unfortunate lady passed away around the year of 1827. Unfortunately, there is no date etched on her gravestone."

Again, Henry Bustle nodded his understanding.

"The year 1830 is significant for two reasons," the Sergeant continued, "It was in that year, according to the parish records in Bermondsey, Gertrude Barratt gave birth to a son, who was Christened, Herbert."

"The same man who presented his mother with the painting of HMS Duke of Wellington and also left flowers on the grave of Elizabeth Barratt, who would have been his grandmother, and who I suspect frequently attends that same grave in Coventry. The man would now be aged around forty-five years."

"But there was another event that took place in 1830. According to the same register in Bermondsey, a daughter was born to a lady by the name of Ann Barnes. That baby was Christened, Rosemary and her father is recorded as being one, Bartholomew Barratt – a forty-five year old Cabinet Maker."

Rayner sat back and exhaled loudly, before acknowledging the scrupulous way in which his Sergeant must have examined those parish records to discover such new and valuable evidence. Rosemary was undoubtedly, Rose Kinley, the third murder victim.

"Did you find any record of Ann Barnes being married to Bartholomew Barratt?" the Inspector asked.

"No, I checked and there is no doubt, there was no marriage that took place."

"So, it appears there were two illegitimate children born that year, and one of them was the aunt of the other?"

"Yes sir. Weird isn't it? But there's more."

Henry Bustle had surprised himself at the amount of information he had gleaned from his travels around London during the day previously. The Sergeant was the kind of man who, once he picked up a trail found it hard to divert away from it. There was no doubt, his efforts had been extremely rewarding. He continued to explain that, whilst searching the Admiralty records, he confirmed that Gertrude's illegitimate son, Herbert, had in fact served as a Junior Lieutenant on HMS Duke of Wellington before being transferred to the Victoria, which was supported by the painting he had sent to his mother. He had left the service in 1862 without giving any forwarding address.

Richard Rayner listened intently, making a mental picture of the relationships between the various members and relatives of the Barratt Family. Then he enquired, "Do we know if Herbert Barratt was associated in anyway with his aunt, Rose Linley?"

"No Inspector, but perhaps Sergeant Pendleton might be able to help us with that one."

"Also, I think we need to know where the Victoria was berthed in 1862 when Herbert Barratt left the service."

"Why should that be important Inspector?" the Sergeant asked.

"Because, not only do we need to trace the man, but it might be useful to speak to anyone who knew Gertrude's son personally, and could give us a reliable description of what he was like. That might just help to give us some indicators which could help us track him down."

The conversation was interrupted by Superintendent Morgan, who stepping into Rayner's office, announced that Ernie Pendleton had just arrested a man at the scene of Rose Linley's murder.

"According to Pendleton, he's the dead woman's brother," the Superintendent declared, "And he's interviewing him downstairs at this very minute."

Both Rayner and Bustle waited outside the ground floor interview room for Sergeant Pendleton to finish his initial enquiries with the prisoner. When he finally appeared, the investigating officer into Rose Linley's murder was shaking his head, obviously not having made any progress.

"Is it okay with you Ernie if we speak with him?" the Inspector asked, more out of polite courtesy towards the man who had made the arrest.

"Go ahead Inspector. He says his name is Jonathan Barnes and claims to be the victim's brother, but he's not telling us much more than that."

"How did you find him?"

"He just turned up at the shop, and when asked, told us who he was. He said that a neighbour had told him about his sister's murder. I will admit though, he does appear to be genuinely distressed so I believe what little he has told us, is true."

Jonathan Barnes was a tall man in his early fifties, with fair hair cut short, showing some grey patches on the sides. He also had a well-trimmed moustache, which added to his distinguished appearance. He was smartly dressed, wearing a brown tweed suit with a rounded collar and cravat, and spoke with an educated voice. Both detectives were surprised when he told them of his current occupation.

"I hold the licence for the Dog and Partridge public house in Minto Street, Bermondsey," the man explained. His reddened eyes bore witness to Sergeant Pendleton's assumption that Barnes had been grieving.

"And you are the brother of Rose Linley?" Rayner asked.

Barnes nodded, before correcting the Inspector. "Half-brother."

"Your mother I take it was, Ann Barnes?"

"Yes."

"And your father's name was?"

"Harvey Barnes, as far as I know. He left my mother when I was very young, and I never really knew him."

Rayner immediately expressed his condolences, and assured the man that everything was being done to apprehend his sister's killer. He then asked if, Jonathan Barnes had any knowledge of Herbert Barratt, who would have been his nephew.

"Yes, I see poor Herbert frequently. He visits us sometimes at the Dog and Partridge and was very close to my mother."

"Do you know where we might find him?" Sergeant Bustle asked.

"He could be anywhere. Herbert's destitute you see. He turns up when he's really hungry and I know he used to pester mother on occasions, asking for food or money."

Rayner was saddened by that particular news, and surprised that a man such as Herbert Barratt, having been a Royal Naval officer, had left the service only to become, what appeared to be, a homeless vagrant living off the streets.

"Tell me Jonathan, do you know of any haunts that Herbert might frequently visit and where we could make a few enquiries?"

"His most visited district is Whitechapel, where he manages to scrape some kind of a living from begging. The problem Herbert has is that he's a drunkard and spends what little money he can beg, or perhaps steal, on drink. The last time I saw him was a couple of days ago, when he called at my establishment and demanded drink. When I refused him, he smashed an empty bottle on the floor, before leaving in a huff and I haven't seen him since."

Rayner then asked whether Barnes knew the two sisters' who used to keep the Tripe Shop in Mount Street, and he confirmed that he used to visit them occasionally, when working as a furrier repairing and cleaning various garments in nearby Oxford Street.

"They never really accepted me, but they were my aunts whether they liked it or not."

"When was the last occasion you saw your aunts' alive?" Henry Bustle asked.

"It was on the day before that terrible incident."

"You mean the day before they were both murdered inside their shop?"

"Yes, I went there with Herbert. He'd been going on about having blood on his hands, but he was always talking like that, so I didn't take much notice at the time. Anyway, I recall he was desperate for money and told me he wanted to sell a painting he'd sent to his mother when he was in the navy, and asked if I would go with him."

"Why was that?" Rayner asked.

"Herbert wanted me to help persuade Gertrude to part with the painting. He was also feeling a little strange about going there I suppose, and felt the need for some support."

The Inspector then asked Barnes to describe his visit to the sisters' shop on that fateful day, in as much detail as he could remember. The man did his utmost to comply with the request. According to his story, both he and Herbert Barratt arrived at the shop after six o'clock that evening, unable to visit earlier because Jonathan couldn't leave his own workplace until that time.

"You see Inspector," he continued, "From the day he was born, Herbert was shunned by his mother and that side of the family. In fact, he was brought up in an orphanage, and I recall my sister took pity on him, buying him small gifts at Christmas and often inviting him to call and see us on occasions. It was my sister who encouraged him to join the navy, and at that time he was a bright lad, who we believed could be successful, which he was when serving. He rose to the rank of lieutenant, before leaving."

"What made him leave the navy?" Henry Bustle asked.

"Who knows. One day he just turned up and told us he'd resigned his commission. He hadn't made any plans and stayed with us for a few weeks before leaving to find work. But that never happened and before too long, I found him standing in some street with a group of other miscreants. They were all drinking from a bottle, and Herbert was still wearing his navy uniform. In fact, he wore nothing else for years."

"So, you abandoned him after seeing what he had lowered himself to?"

"No; I was disappointed to see such a fine young man turn to the bottle, but I've always tried to look after him whenever I could, and always gave him advice, telling him of various work opportunities; but alas, he was only ever interested in drink."

Richard Rayner took back control of the interview and asked Barnes to recollect what took place during the visit to the sisters' shop.

The man recalled that, when Herbert asked for the return of his painting of HMS Duke of Wellington, his mother Gertrude refused, and there was an argument. He also explained that, although during the earlier years, Herbert had tried incessantly to contact his mother, there was never any response. According to Jonathan, they remained with the two sisters' for some considerable time, with Herbert making it clear that he had never asked for anything from his mother or her family during his lifetime, but was now so desperate for help, the only way he could raise money was by selling the painting he had brought for her, and which was hanging on the wall of the parlour.

"You mention there was an argument between Herbert and I take it, his mother."

"Yes."

"A violent argument, would you say?"

"No Inspector, there was no physical contact, only heated words. In any case, Aunt Gertrude was adamant she was not going to part with the picture, so that was the end of it."

"Was any other subject discussed during your visit there?" Rayner asked.

"Oh yes, Herbert was determined to give a full account of his lifetime of suffering, but I recall he tried to elicit some pride from his mother when he talked about his life in the navy. Aunt Gertrude however, didn't seem to be interested and eventually, when the argument became heated, she actually threatened to call for a policeman to have him thrown off the premises."

"And what role did the other sister Emily play, while all of this was going on?"

"Like myself, she sat quietly, just being an observer really and occasionally supporting her sister. I was of the opinion that Gertrude was the stronger of the two and didn't really need any help, but I must admit to being a little dismayed at the way she treated her own son, even if he'd been born out of wedlock."

Jonathan Barnes's resume of the events of that evening fifteen years previously, had an element of truth and Rayner believed every word the man spoke. But there were other issues he needed to deal with.

"What time did you leave your aunts' shop that evening Jonathan?"

"Oh, it was late, well after midnight as I wanted to get home because of work the following morning. I remember I was tired and hungry. My aunts' hadn't offered us any food or refreshments all the time we were there."

"And Herbert left with you?"

"No, I persisted in telling him I needed to leave, but he was so engrossed in telling Gertrude how he had missed a mother's love and now needed some kind of support, he stayed and I left him there with the two ladies."

Henry Bustle stood from his seat and stepped across to the far wall of the interview room, before asking, "You mentioned that Herbert told you he had blood on his hands. Was that before or after the visit you paid to the sisters' shop?"

"He was always saying daft things like that, before that visit and several times after it."

"Do you think that Herbert could have been responsible for their murders?"

Jonathan Barnes hesitated before answering, and finally agreed, "I suppose he could, but Gertrude was his mother and there was no doubt in my mind that he loved her dearly, although that love was never returned. I think that Herbert could commit such atrocious acts when in temper, but I would never believe he would kill his own mother or family if it came to that, even when in drink."

Chapter Seventeen

Constable Jack Robinson felt somewhat strangely disorientated, as he entered Scotland Yard through the front entrance. It was his first day back at work; a day which he had been looking forward to for weeks, and now it had finally arrived, the young man felt almost overwhelmed by apprehension. However, such debilitating emotion did not last long, and after nervously stepping into Richard Rayner's office, after tapping on the door, the return of the Prodigal Son was warmly greeted by both the Inspector and Sergeant Bustle. Handshakes and pats on the back were all that Jack required to break the ice, and make him feel welcome once again. When Superintendent Morgan joined the small welcoming party, his gesture of cordiality was the icing on the cake.

Having had plenty of time to consider his future and having been visited several times by Lizzie Donogue when recuperating in hospital, accompanied by their baby son on each occasion, Constable Robinson had discovered that he was in love after all. The decision of betrothal had been made final. It was to be a Spring Wedding and arrangements were already being made, including invitations being sent to each of his work colleagues who were all genuinely pleased for the man, after what he'd been through recently.

Once the celebrations had died down, the detectives returned to their top priority which was to urgently discover the whereabouts of Herbert Barratt, whose name had now been moved to the very top of their list of suspects.

Covent Garden was yet another fruit and vegetable stronghold from which traders sold their produce. Similar to Smithfield, it was always crammed with people, some of whom patiently searched for bargains, others less patient when looking for a candidate to rob or steal from. Just four years earlier, the impressive neo-classical building had been topped by a roof, giving the whole market structure a more permanent appearance. As a result, many of the traders decided to live close by, bringing an end to a middle-class district, as its former inhabitants were squeezed out to seek residences further afield.

Amongst those offering their goods for sale was non more prolific than a flower seller by the name of Alice Burns. She was a robust Glaswegian lady whose presence was always marked by the loud echo of a trumpet sounding voice that could be heard over the surrounding din created by other vociferous traders. Scots Alice, as she was commonly known as, had been a stalwart of the market since its most recent building had been erected some twenty-five years beforehand. During that time, she had frequently recruited small armies of homeless street urchins, which she referred to as her family. Each member was highly skilled in relieving visitors to Covent Garden of their valuables and personal effects.

The central figure in the daily drama that took place within the market walls, would pay pennies to each of her family members, in return for what products they had managed to rob or steal. It was when she was exchanging a little brass for an expensive woman's necklace with one of her ragamuffin's, that she noticed Detective Sergeant Henry Bustle approaching from the main entrance.

"Scarper and be quick about it," she gasped at the boy, snatching the stolen piece of jewelry from his hand, before it rapidly disappeared to somewhere on her voluminous person. The lad with the dirty face and snotty nose needed no second invitation, and was gone in a flash.

"Good day to you, Alice," Bustle said, tipping his hat to the flower seller, "Perhaps you would like me to take a look at that necklace you've just taken from young Nobby Scratch, just to make sure it hasn't been nicked?"

"Necklace, Mr. Bustle? Necklace?" she bawled out, before roaring in laughter with both hands on hips that were invisible to the naked eye, and rocking her flabby frame to and fro.

It was a diversionary tactic the Sergeant had seen many times before, so he just stood there and waited for the woman to settle down once again.

"Better still, Alice, why don't I summon that Peeler over there to help me strip you down, and search those ship's masts you call draws, and recover that necklace myself."

"You wouldn't dare, you fornicating bastard," she challenged, trying hard to arch her back in defiance, at the same time filling her huge cheeks with air.

"Perhaps not woman," Bustle answered, smiling mischievously, "I can think of something better I require."

Alice turned her back on the Sergeant and maneuvered her way back behind her stall, like a swaying Hippopotamus caught in a gale. Then, facing her unwelcome visitor, she enquired in a quieter voice, "How can I help you Mr. Bustle?"

"Herbert Barratt, Alice. A nomad who drinks a lot."

"Don't they all."

"This one comes from good stock and has spent a few years now living on the cobbles. He used to be a naval officer and I'm sure the man wouldn't hold back in telling everybody about his former life, for a bottle or two of rotgut. His mother and aunt were murdered over in Whitechapel about fifteen years ago. Ring any bells?"

Alice Burns nodded her head and rolled her eyes towards the overcast sky.

"How much?" she asked.

"Your continued liberty, and of course whatever you can get for that sparkling item stuck down your draws."

"You surely are Lucifer's disciple," she snapped at her visitor, "And if your britches got any tighter, your bollocks would pop out." Again, a bout of raucous laughter echoed around the Market Hall, forcing the Sergeant to wait another few seconds before getting his answer.

"He hangs about in Whitechapel; a poor soul who lives for his gin, or anything else that would ease him from his nightmares."

"Any locality in particular?"

"You said yourself, he's a vagrant, but if I was a betting lady, which I'm not, I would put my stall and all of these here green stalks on him visiting the soup kitchens."

"Which one?" It was like drawing teeth, but Henry Bustle was well acquainted with the delaying game usually played by those offering him any snippet that might be beneficial.

"I would favour the one at the back of St Mary's in Whitechapel High Street. I've heard he does odd jobs now and again for that walking stick who calls himself the Reverend Mitchell."

"Thank you, Alice," Bustle said, tipping his hat once more, before turning to leave. As he was making his way through the crowds, he could hear the woman growling before breaking into a rendition of, "Bunches of Flowers for a copper each."

Inspector Rayner had decided to initially concentrate on the Whitechapel District of London, having been guided by the information volunteered by the man's uncle, Jonathan Barnes. The description of Barratt, provided by Barnes was circulated to the beat men, and Rayner intended to visit the soup kitchens in person, whilst Henry Bustle was probing whatever informants he could find across London. The services of Jack Robinson were also put to good use by the Inspector, who instructed the young constable to attend to the other local charities in the district, including the parish churches. It was Rayner's desire not to subject the young man to any kind of violent confrontation on his first day back on duty, and by keeping him distanced from his Sergeant, there would be a lesser chance of that happening.

Herbert Barratt was described as being a forty-five year old man, of average height and thinly built. According to Barnes, his nephew had dark straggly hair, the ends of which touched his shoulders and a complexion that was as white as the snow outside. Other features were that Barratt's dark eyes had become sunken, and he always had a fairly heavy stubble across the lower part of his face.

Rayner sought out people who were responsible for the soup kitchens that were located in a wider area surrounding Whitechapel, whilst Jack Robinson followed the same route he had taken when the search for Peter the Tinman was ongoing. When he returned to St Mary's Church in Adler Street, he found the Reverend Walter Mitchell, kneeling at his altar.

The white haired, spindly parson turned when he heard Jack's footsteps approaching from behind, and stood to greet the young constable.

Jack immediately apologised for disturbing the man of the cloth, but Reverend Mitchell was unperturbed, offering the constable a pew before sitting next to him.

"I heard that you had some success in finding Peter the Tinman and how sad that turned out to be," the parson remarked.

"It was tragic vicar; he took his own life."

"And he will be damned forever my son, for committing such an atrocity against God's Law."

"From what I learned of him, the man was damned throughout his life on Earth in any case."

"Sadly, so I understand. So how can I help you now constable?"

Jack named the man he was looking for and reverberated Herbert Barratt's description to the parson, before explaining, "We need to locate him urgently vicar, in connection with the same case in which the Tinman was suspected."

"We have recently opened a soup kitchen at the back of the church, which accommodates the homeless every Tuesday and Friday evenings between six and nine. Fortunately, we have a few good-hearted women who volunteer to run the kitchen for us, and we can but pray that further support will be forthcoming in the near future."

"To your knowledge sir, have you seen anyone answering that description attend at your kitchen?" Jack enquired.

"Yes, I do believe we have one gentlemen of the road, who attends. He is about the same age with long dark hair that reaches his shoulders, and I do believe I have heard one of our women call him Bert, if that sounds familiar to you?"

"It could be our man vicar. Does this individual attend on both nights or one in particular?"

"Well now, let me see. As with all of our homeless parishioners, I should imagine he attends whenever there is an opportunity to seek sustenance, which means he could be with us this very evening, as it's indeed Tuesday."

"Might I see where the kitchen is situated?"

"Of course constable, but if it is the man you seek, then I can only pray that he doesn't commit suicide in similar fashion to the last man you were enquiring about."

The vicar then led Jack Robinson outside and up a narrow pathway which ran the length of the dilapidated church, until they reached a small enclosed red bricked courtyard at the back. There was a small wooden hut situated in one corner, with an opening through which the soup was served.

"Unfortunately, we have not yet been able to provide any seating for our recipients," the vicar confessed, "But we hope to very soon."

"So, what do the vagrants do? I mean do they just stand there and drink their soup or perhaps sit on the ground?"

"In such foul weather as this, it is advisable for them to remain on their feet and once they have emptied their bowls, they return them to the ladies."

"Six o'clock tonight you say, vicar?"

"We open the kitchen at six and close it at nine, or within reason if there are still customers to be served, and of course provided we have some soup left for them, but the majority of our visitors attend during the first hour."

Once again, Jack thanked the Reverend before scuttling back to Scotland Yard to share his news with the others. If the man the parson had mentioned turned out to be Herbert Barratt, then it would be a feather in the young constable's cap. Unfortunately, when he arrived back at the Yard, both Rayner and Bustle were still out making their own enquires, so rather than wait Jack decided to disclose what he had learned to Superintendent Morgan, in fear of the time running out.

"Well done lad," the Superintendent loudly spoke, congratulating the constable, "If the Inspector or Sergeant haven't returned by four o'clock then come back to me, and we will make some contingency plans."

Jack returned to the Inspector's office and patiently waited, hoping that Richard Rayner would return before the deadline set by Morgan. One thing that the constable wasn't looking forward to, was having to go on an operation with the domineering Superintendent. Although Frederick Morgan had always treated Jack fairly, the young man still felt nervous when in his presence. As it so happened, young Robinson's anxieties were proved to be unfounded as the Inspector returned earlier than anticipated, having completed his own enquiries without success.

Rayner sat and listened to the young constable's report and then commented on the fact that the Reverend Walter Mitchell was only going on the description given to him, which he felt might not be sufficiently conclusive.

"One of the women also called the man 'Bert' sir, which could be short for Herbert," Jack suggested.

"Yes, that could be the case," the Inspector agreed, sitting back in his chair and obviously giving a great deal of thought to this latest information. "Well young Jack, it's all we have to go on at the moment, so if Sergeant Bustle hasn't returned by the time we leave, it will be you and I who will visit St Mary's. You know Jack, I have a feeling you might be on the right track with this one."

"Thank you sir."

Chapter Eighteen

Herbert Barratt was a slave to the gin bottle. Throughout his turbulent but lonely life, all he had asked for; begged for, was some recognition of his existence from his mother. Having been abandoned at birth and raised in an orphanage, the destitute young man had been self-educated to quite a high level, requiring some tutorial support from a clergyman who had shown some interest in his pupil's wellbeing and future.

Throughout that period of learning, the youngster had worked for a blacksmith before constantly dripping with sweat as a furnace worker in a number of factories. He had even toiled on various building sites, saving every penny he earned. Finally, and again with some assistance from the same clergy man who had helped with his reading and understanding of the world, Herbert had sufficient funds to buy a commission in the Royal Navy. Eventually, he served as a Junior Lieutenant on HMS Victoria. All of this was an attempt to earn some kind of affection from Gertrude Barratt, and yet he was still alienated by his mother and other members of her family, destined to remain an outcast.

The young man, following an incident when on shore leave, became despondent and frustrated. He resigned his commission and took to a life where his only companion came from a bottle of spirit, living on the streets and scrapping for every coin he could lay his hands on in order to maintain his habit. After years of trying to extract a mother's love, he eventually accepted that, in the eyes of the lady he had devoted his life towards obtaining the merest recognition, he was invisible to those who he believed should have opened their doors to him.

The only two people who had showed some kind of interest in the forsaken man, was his Aunt, Rose Kinley and her step brother, Jonathan Barnes. But now there was nobody and Herbert Barratt concentrated his mind only on surviving and drinking as much alcohol as was necessary to blunt the chronic depression from which he suffered.

As he stood at the back of the queue at St Mary's soup kitchen that cold and frosty evening, all the lessons he had learned from having been a vagrant on the streets of London, suddenly came together to sound alarm bells from within his half-stupefied senses. His guilty mind had at least failed to blunt the sharpness of his sensitivities. Something was not right and voices were now telling him that what little was left of a miserable future, was now in danger.

Grasping tightly on to a half empty bottle in one pocket of an oversized overcoat he was wearing, he felt like he was standing on a railway track with a steam locomotive heading his way. Keeping his head lowered, his reddened eyes glanced around in all directions, in search of that train which was about to deliver him into the jaws of Hell.

When the queue moved forward, the smell of hot soup became stronger, and the vagrant's stomach began to remind him that his leaning towards gin was insufficient to nourish his inner self. And yet, the warning signals persisted and he continued to watch, like a young Raven being stalked by some alley cat.

By the time he was within a pace of what would be his life line for the next twenty-four hours, the female servers' voices were louder, and the inviting smell of hot nourishment was more intense. Then he noticed a man dressed in the kind of clothing that was at odds with his surroundings. The man appeared from behind the shed from which the soup was being served and stood at the side. He was dressed like a well-heeled gentleman, neither vagrant or clergy.

Herbert glanced back and immediately noticed another, much younger man, standing to one side between his position and the pathway down which he had just trod. Even under the influence of alcohol, the vagrant still retained his senses, and recognised instantly that the two men had to be peelers. He would not be participating in his evening meal on this occasion, and all he could think of was escape. Fleeing from where the two men were so obviously intent on taking him off the streets. Through the mists of his confusion, he decided there was only one course of action to take.

Richard Rayner slowly moved towards the wanted man, nodding towards Jack Robinson to do the same.

Suddenly, as both detectives drew closer, Barratt produced a handgun and pointed it in the direction of Constable Robinson. No words were spoken, but Herbert's hostile action was sufficient for Jack to step to one side, as the vagrant moved menacingly towards him, the barrel of the gun leading the way.

"Don't be a fool, Herbert," the young constable quietly said, as the suspect drew nearer, waving the barrel to signal the officer to get down on the snow-covered ground.

"Stay where you are Mr. Barratt," the Inspector yelled from behind the suspect, "We only want to talk to you."

Herbert immediately swiveled round and fired his gun, the bullet flying over Rayner's head, forcing the Inspector to hit the ground.

The queue became fractured, and the other vagrants and the two women inside the shed screamed out in protest. All frightened eyes watched as the armed man swept past Jack Robinson, before fleeing down the side of the church, still grasping his gun in one hand.

Once he reached the street, Herbert turned right along Whitechapel High Street, but slipped on the icy paving before regaining his feet. Looking over his shoulder he could see the two detectives running towards him. He fired yet another shot, which thankfully missed his target. The fugitive then leapt across the recently fallen snow, heading towards his own safe haven which consisted of a network of narrow alleyways within the heart of the Whitechapel District.

The vagrant continued waving his gun, as a man wearing a heavy coat walked towards him. On seeing the gunman, the pedestrian held both arms up in the air in surrender, before stepping to one side, inviting the runner to pass by without hindrance.

Herbert Barratt was desperate to reach the inner warren of Whitechapel and the panic in his eyes reflected just that. There could be little doubt, if anyone tried to obstruct the man, they would be shot without hesitation.

As he attempted to fly past the man in the heavy coat, who was still standing motionless at one side of the pavement, a hand suddenly shot out and grasped Herbert's gun hand, with the other fist landing in his stomach. The murder suspect doubled up, groaning and allowing his assailant to wrench the firearm from him, before using the butt to hit him over the back of his head. He collapsed down on to the snow covered paving slabs having been rendered harmless.

When Richard Rayner and Jack Robinson reached the fallen suspect, Henry Bustle was placing a pair of heavy shackles on both his prisoner's wrists.

"Henry," gasped the Inspector, but before he could ask the obvious question, the Sergeant quickly related what he had found out from Scots Alice in Covent Garden. He also explained that, having been told by Superintendent Morgan where his colleagues had disappeared to, he was just making his way towards them when he happened to bump into the very man they had been searching for.

"Well, I must say Henry, your timing is impeccable."

After the prisoner had been secured in a downstairs cell, the Superintendent joined his three officers in the Inspectors office, insisting that he be allowed to top up their mugs of tea with some find brandy.

Morgan was in a celebratory mood.

Although his colleagues appeared to be overjoyed by the evening's achievement, in contrast to their optimism, Richard Rayner remained reserved. When asked by the Superintendent for the reasons for his obvious concern, the Inspector explained they first needed to listen to what the prisoner was likely to tell them, before considering any possible charge.

"He looks a wretched soul, Superintendent," Rayner explained, "And it appears obvious the man is in need of medical treatment."

"But not before you have spoken to him. The fact that he served in Her Majesty's navy, doesn't give him the right to fire a pistol at any of my officers, and for that course of action, hospital treatment or not, he will pay dearly."

"Let's see what he has to say about being charged with the attempted murder of two Scotland Yard police officers," Henry Bustle remarked.

"Yes Henry, let's go and listen to exactly what he has to tell us," Rayner answered, nodding for the Sergeant to follow him to the interview room.

Herbert Barratt was still in shackles when the Inspector invited him to take a seat. Rayner had already tasked Constable Robinson with bringing the prisoner a hot meal and tea, before giving notice to the prisoner that he was about to be fed.

Barratt sat with his head lowered and both cuffed wrists resting on his lap, obviously totally dejected. It would only take a cup of gin to revive the man completely, but Richard Rayner's charity would never go that far.

After introducing himself and Sergeant Bustle, the first question Rayner asked was when had Herbert Barratt last seen his mother, Gertrude Barratt, alive.

The alcoholic looked up, as though peering through a haze of smoke at the Inspector, and initially declined to speak.

"Herbert, we have been talking to your uncle, Jonathan Barnes and are well aware of the atrocities you have committed."

"He's a good man," the prisoner answered quietly, addressing the floor with his answer.

"As you once were from what I understand. An officer on HMS Victoria, to living the kind of life you lead now."

The prisoner looked away and began to shake his head. There was a cloak of shame hanging over him, invisible to the naked eye but one that could be easily seen.

Rayner needed some kind of topic with which to trigger the man's desire to speak openly. From what Barnes had told them previously, the former naval officer had spent most of his life trying hard to get his own mother to recognise him, so the Inspector decided that was the path to follow.

"I understand your mother was extremely cruel to you, failing to acknowledge that you were actually alive," he said, awaiting a response with enthusiasm. What Rayner was anticipating, came without hesitation.

Barratt glared at him, his reddened eyes filled with hostility and hatred.

"My mother was not cruel, you lying bastard," he screamed out, "My mother was the most loving lady in the world."

"Then tell me Herbert, why did you batter her to death, and also brutally murder your Aunt Emily in their Tripe shop that night, some fifteen years ago?" Rayner had to raise his voice to penetrate through the suspect's wall of rage, "Just tell me why you did those things?"

"So that's what you think is it?" the man answered, calming down and sitting back in his chair, "You honestly think that I murdered my own beloved mother?"

"Well, all the evidence seems to point in that direction Herbert."

"Well you are wrong and I would never have harmed a hair on my mother's head. I loved my mother."

"What about your Aunt Emily?" Bustle asked, "Did you love her as well, or just batter her to death for the fun of it?"

The prisoner snarled at the Sergeant and slammed both manacled hands on top of the desk in anguish.

Henry Bustle immediately responded by standing from his seat and lifting a fist in the air, obviously intent on slamming it into the prisoner's face, but was quickly stopped by his Inspector.

"Sit down Henry," Rayner ordered, before turning to Barratt and explaining, "Losing your temper will not be to your benefit Herbert. You are already facing serious charges of attempted murder of two police officers when you fired that gun at us, so I suggest you try and use that head of yours, the one that used to think logically and intelligently, before your fall from grace sir." Rayner put some emphasis on the word, 'sir' suspecting it might recall some more calming memories for the man, particularly when he was a naval officer. It seemed to work and the vitriolic look in Barratt's eyes disappeared.

Once the prisoner became more pacified, the Inspector continued by asking, "Have you blood on your hands Herbert and please answer me truthfully."

Much to both detectives' surprise, their man nodded his head, but remained silent.

"Why is that, I am wondering. Are you thinking about some incident that took place during your distinguished navy days?"

Again, Barratt nodded his head.

"Then why should you think such a thing?"

"Because I have blood on my hands. My mother and aunt were both murdered brutally, and it might just as well have been me that done for them."

"I do not understand what you are saying," Rayner quietly admitted, "Enlighten me Herbert."

The prisoner again retreated behind his wall of silence, just as there was a knock on the door and Jack Robinson entered carrying a tray containing a hot meal and mug of tea. The enforced break was inconvenient, but Rayner thought it necessary, leaving the prisoner to have his fill.

Chapter Nineteen

The sun reflected off the vines, as the small pony and trap maneuvered its way down one of the many dividing lines, heading towards the large house at the top of the hill. The horse was tired, following the journey back from Lyon and so was the driver. When they arrived at the foot of a set of marble steps leading up to the front door, a stable boy appeared and took the reins from his master, who then hurriedly entered the building, carrying a parcel beneath an arm.

Once inside the house, he proceeded into the ground floor library where he placed the package on a small corner table, before opening it with a glint of pride in both eyes. Inside a brightly polished Cherry wood box, was a pair of dueling pistols, together with all the necessary accessories required for maintaining the weapons.

The man stood for a moment, admiring his latest acquisition which had been expertly made to his own requirements, and felt the softness of the velvet inlay. He then carefully held each pistol in turn, noticing the excellent balance and comfortable grip; pulling back the hammers, before listening with enthusiasm to the clicks produced as the triggers were levered back. That afternoon would be spent practicing with live ammunition, and his self-confidence now soared, causing him to smile arrogantly in the belief he remained safe from the clutches of the English Detective Inspector.

"If you want my opinion Inspector," Henry Bustle put forward, "The man's not all there, and he talks in riddles."

They were sitting in Richard Rayner's office, and Superintendent Morgan had just joined them.

"A mad man, eh?" Frederick Morgan assumed, "That's more reason why he could have bashed his own mother's head in, don't you think?"

"I find it difficult to accept Herbert Barratt is mad," Rayner answered, "Of course, he's a man in despair and perhaps a little unbalanced, which is not surprising considering the kind of life he's led, but I truly believe he has all his faculties."

"Then why is he denying the murders one minute, and then admitting responsibility the next?" asked the Sergeant.

"He's not admitting actually committing the murders Henry, he is talking as though he knows who did, and is fearful that in some way he is distantly responsible."

"He sounds like a mad man to me," Morgan remarked.

Rayner took a drink from his mug of tea provided by Constable Robinson, and leant back in his seat, gazing up at the ceiling.

"He has a secret which he appears to be scared of sharing with us. In fact, it's my guess that whatever particle of knowledge that is, which seems to have been gnawing away at him, it has been present over the past fifteen years, and could be the reason for him turning to the drink and falling from grace."

"Then what's your next move Inspector?" asked the Superintendent.

"To prise it from him, but we won't do that by the use of violence," Rayner suggested, looking directly at Henry Bustle, "We need patience now gentlemen, and we need to coax it from him."

"The Commissioner is aware of the arrest and is anxious for some news," Morgan explained, "What shall I tell him?"

"The truth," the Inspector recommended, "That we are still interviewing the man." At that, Rayner finished his tea and made for the door, anxious to return back to the interview room.

As he and Sergeant Bustle made their way back down to the cell block where the interview room was located, the Inspector stopped and looked towards his colleague.

"Charlie Walker, the delivery man, told me that he dropped off that final delivery during the morning of the day prior to the murders being committed."

"So?"

"Charlie then mentioned that he had followed Emily Barratt into the parlour and saw a man wearing bell bottom trousers, sitting on the sofa there."

"According to what Jonathan Barnes told us, that could not have been Herbert Barratt, as they didn't visit the sisters' shop until six o'clock that evening, after he had finished work."

Rayner smiled and said, "We need to confirm that with our Mr.

Barratt."

They found the prisoner still sitting in the same position as when they had earlier left him. Barratt looked more content, having just devoured the meal provided, and the constable posted to remain in attendance with the manacled man, was dismissed by the Inspector.

Richard Rayner sat in silence, scrutinising the prisoner who was staring down at the table top, breathing noisily and obviously anticipating the questions about to be asked. In a strange way, the Inspector was feeling some sympathy towards the man, now realising how difficult it must have been for him, knowing he had a mother who wanted nothing to do with her son. By her unacceptable behaviour, Gertrude Barratt had been guilty of mental cruelty when refusing to even acknowledge her son's existence.

"I appreciate you have lived a rather tortuous existence Herbert," the Inspector confessed, "And the fact that you were so desperate to receive some warmth and understanding from your mother, only to be denied those natural emotions, must have been soul destroying for you."

The prisoner still remained staring down at the table top, and Rayner heard his Sergeant shuffle about in his seat, obviously impatient to move the interview on. He silently held up a hand signalling that he wanted no interference at that moment. Equanimity was the preferred and essential calmness required.

"Have you ever tried to reason why your mother acted in the manner she did?" he asked quietly.

Finally, Barratt confirmed he had been listening to what Richard

Rayner had been saying, by looking up and replying, "It was the others. She was afraid that the other members of her family would condemn her more if she showed me any affection. But I knew deep down, she loved me."

"When you visited your mother on that dreadful night, together with your uncle, Jonathan Barnes, was that the first time you had been to that shop?"

"I called there some time before that, and stood in the shop looking at her, but it was as though she didn't recognise me, and Aunt Emily told me to leave, so I did."

"I mean earlier on that day, the same day before you went there with your uncle."

The prisoner shook his head, but then seemed to recall an earlier event.

"I did call to see her that morning on my own. I was desperate for money and hoped that she would give me something."

"What happened on that occasion?"

"Nothing. I sat talking to her while Aunt Emily minded the shop out front and begged her for money, but she was adamant she wouldn't give me a penny. I asked if I could have the painting of my ship back so I could sell it, and she refused." He paused to look at both detectives, before continuing, "She told me that she did not want to see me ever again."

"Was there any kind of struggle or assault took place on that occasion?" the Inspector asked.

Barratt looked confused by the question and shook his head.

"No, I never laid a hand on her. I never would."

"Did she assault you in anyway?"

"Only when she first asked me to leave, and I refused to go until she gave me the painting."

Rayner than produced the button he'd recovered from Albert Greening and enquired, "Have you seen this before Herbert?"

"My mother snatched it off my jacket when we were arguing. I thought I had lost it."

Rayner could see the pain in the man's eyes and begged to know, what had taken place after that first, earlier skirmish.

"I eventually left and that's why I went to see Jonathan at his place of work, which was in Oxford Street, and asked if he would return to the shop with me and try and persuade my mother to let me have the painting back."

Rayner sat back, knowing the man was telling the truth. Everything he had said about that final visit to the Tripe Shop in Mount Street had been confirmed by Jonathan Barnes.

Henry Bustle's grating voice then filled the room, when he spoke for the first time, "Why do you believe you have blood on your hands Herbert? Have you killed anybody since leaving the navy?"

The prisoner bowed his head once more without answering, but then to the surprise of both detectives, began to weep. They both sat there watching him, as he wiped his eyes with the back of his manacled hands. But Henry Bustle was like a starving dog with a bone, and was not prepared to let his question remain unanswered. He repeated it.

Herbert Barratt suddenly looked up with tears streaming down his face, and out of nowhere confessed to knowing who the killer of his mother and aunt was.

"It was his revenge for what I did to his family in France, all those years ago," he blurted out.

This was exactly what Richard Rayner had been hoping for, and he sat back listening intently, as the man's story began to unfold. Now that the prisoner was talking, it would be folly to interrupt him and Henry Bustle was also aware of that fact.

Some sixteen years earlier in 1859, the same year as Herbert Barratt resigned his commission, his ship HMS Victoria was berthed just off Marseille. Some of the officers were granted shore leave whilst the vessel had necessary repairs undertaken, at the same time, taking on board various supplies. The Victoria was expected to remain in the Mediterranean Sea for at least one week, allowing plenty of time for most of the ship's company and officers to enjoy their furlough in Marseilles.

Up until then, Junior Lieutenant Barratt drank very little alcohol, excepting of course his daily ration of rum. It was on the second day ashore that the Englishman met up with a small group of Frenchmen, one in particular who gave his name as, Francis Colbert, a former Legionnaire in the French Foreign Legion. The two men, one from either side of the English Channel, quickly became friends and Barratt soon became impressed by Colbert's boasts of having a vineyard just outside Saint-Priest, which was close to the city of Lyon. In fact, having shared a large number of bottles of local wine in a Marseille hostelry, the Englishman was invited to visit the former Legionnaire's estate.

They travelled through the night, until reaching Colbert's home, where the English Lieutenant was introduced to both his host's wife, Maria and the couple's young son, Rafal.

The former Legionnaire was the perfect host, but the young Herbert Barratt soon faced a self-inflicted problem. He fell in love with Maria Colbert and his feelings were quickly reciprocated. During the short time the man from the Victoria stayed at the Chateau, the couple used every devious method they could create to spend time alone, until the inevitable happened and the lady's husband became suspicious.

Finally, one day Francis Colbert took his son out hunting for game, leaving the way clear for his wife and English guest to spend time in bed. They made passionate love throughout the morning and afternoon, until their lustful association was interrupted by the master of the house finding them in bed together. Colbert had quite deliberately returned from his hunting trip with his son, earlier than had been anticipated.

There followed a violent altercation, and an enraged vineyard owner shot his wife dead where she lay on the marriage bed. Turning to subject his English guest to the same fatality, Herbert was already racing from the building with his clothes huddled together in his arms.

"Your bad luck appears to have followed you even to France," Henry Bustle remarked.

"The last thing I heard Monsieur Colbert screaming from the

bedroom window, was that he would avenge the death of his wife, having blamed me for his loss of self-control. I thought he would have been dealt with by the French for the murder of his wife, until I saw him here in London, just prior to the murders of my mother and aunt."

"Where was this?" asked Rayner.

"In Whitechapel. He didn't see me, but I saw him walking towards Turner Street, near to the hospital. He had a hood over his head, but I easily recognised him. I didn't think at the time he would even know where my mother lived."

"Was it that event which took place in Saint-Priest, the reason why you left the navy?"

"Yes, as soon as we returned from the Mediterranean to Portsmouth, I resigned my Commission."

Richard Rayner looked across at his Sergeant, who nodded his head, signalling that he believed the prisoner's story. He then turned back to, Herbert Barratt and asked one further question.

"Then, tell me Herbert, who was responsible for the more recent murder of your Aunt, Rose Kinley?" He strongly suspected the former naval officer knew something about that incident, and now the man was pouring his heart out, decided it was the right time to press home the matter.

Barratt once again looked down at the table top and shook his head.

"Why did you have to kill Rose, Herbert?" the Inspector asked, pointedly.

Henry Bustle looked sharply across at Rayner, not having had the slightest suspicion that the man before them had committed that particular atrocity. The Sergeant remained silent though, and waited for the prisoner's response.

The man glanced up with more tears in his eyes. "Aunt Rose always suspected that I had killed my mother. She was wrong, and although she never said so, I always felt there was some distance between us following those murders."

"So, what was your reason for killing her, and please do not insult us by suggesting it would have been Francis Colbert who was the man responsible."

"Then who else would have murdered my mother and Aunt so brutally, to satisfy his lust for revenge?"

"I am talking about the death of your Aunt Rose."

"I called to see her and asked for money. I was desperate, but she refused, just as my mother had done all those years before. She told me how much she was ashamed of me and that I had become a pitiful drunkard who had no future. I continued to beg and plead with her, and we argued."

"Go on, Herbert."

"I only meant to frighten her into giving me some money, and grabbed her round her neck." He paused and looked at Rayner with a confused expression.

"What happened then?"

Barratt winced and his voice became excitable.

"I must have lost control, because the next thing I knew, I was standing over her, holding a brass candle stick in one hand, covered in blood."

"What did you do then?"

"Nothing. I ran out through the front door before her girl helper returned from where ever it was my Aunt had sent her."

"Did you not think to stay and help your aunt?"

He shook his head. "No, I knew she was already dead."

"What did you do with the candlestick?"

"I cleaned it and tried to sell it, but no one was interested. I couldn't even persuade the pawnbroker in Whitechapel Street to take it off my hands, so I eventually threw it into the docks by the North Quay."

Richard Rayner stood for a moment, still feeling some sympathy towards a man whose mind had been driven by the unsuppressed craving for alcohol, which had undoubtedly encouraged such a violent disposition.

Henry Bustle could only see in his mind, the noose that was going to be placed around the killer's neck.

"Have you any regrets about killing your Aunt in cold blood?" Rayner asked,

"Of course I do. It happened in a fit of temper."

After escorting their prisoner to a cell, both detectives returned to Richard Rayner's office in silence, and where Superintendent Morgan was waiting for them.

The Inspector updated him on what Herbert Barratt had told them, including his confession for having committed the most recent murder. It was obvious that Morgan was itching to climb the stairs to inform the Commissioner that finally, his department was responsible for capturing someone for the murder of Rose Kinley. But before he left, he turned and addressed both officers by acknowledging, "You both best get packed then. It looks like you will be soon crossing the Channel to complete the Inquiry in the South of France. I want that Frog brought back here to face the hangman. Is that understood." Frederick Morgan was back to his normal domineering self.

Chapter Twenty

Calais was a bustling port, seemingly overcrowded and extremely noisy, as the two English detectives discovered when they finally arrived, and cautiously made their way down the wooden gang plank to disembark on to the quayside.

Henry Bustle looked slightly ashen, having been incapable of stopping the constant bouts of sickness throughout the complete crossing. In fact, as soon as the ferry had left Dover the Sergeant had immediately taken up a position at a rail towards the front of the boat, and never moved from there. That was until they had reached the calm waters of the French harbour. He thanked the Lord for having been safely returned to dry land, having often thought his life was about to expire during the short period of time they had been at sea.

Richard Rayner remained his usual halcyon self, smartly dressed and wearing a brown silk top hat. The Inspector stood erect, still taking deep breaths of the sea air, whilst indulging in the wondrous sights of such a busy and industrious coastal fishing port. Each of the English visitors was carrying a small travel companion, both containing amongst their individual change of clothing and other requirements, a pair of iron shackles, in readiness for the arrest they intended to make on French soil. Of course, they would have to approach any deportation with sensitivity, knowing they would require the French Authorities to consent to the removal of one of their citizens from the country. Rayner had already considered that problem and was relying on full French co-operation. He was also aware there was no guarantee that would be the case, albeit England had not warred with France since the conflicts resulting during the Napoleonic era.

After obtaining directions to the Rue Royale, where the Headquarters of the Gendarmerie Nationale was situated, the Scotland Yard detectives set out from the port on foot. As they progressed into the town, they encountered an atmosphere of sheer pandemonium. A multitude of honking horns; galloping horses pulling various designs of carriages; men carrying heavy boxes on their shoulders; ladies moving gracefully beneath hand held parasols, greeted them. Then there was just about every breed of dog known to man, scampering about the narrow-cobbled streets in search of any morsel they could devour. It seemed that Calais was a menagerie of total confusion and dis-organised activities.

"It's nothing like London Inspector," Sergeant Bustle remarked flippantly.

"Of course not Henry. It's Calais and it's French."

The two visitors soon completed the short walk, finally arriving at what they found to be an impressive multi-storey building, reaching higher than the surrounding flat roofed dwellings of the port.

There they were greeted by a man who introduced himself as being

Lieutenant Edvard Moreau, who fortunately for the visitors, could speak reasonable English. He was a short, stocky man with fashionable mutton chop whiskers on each side of his face. He displayed a large gold watch chain that stretched across the front of his olive-green waistcoat, the same colour as the checked suit he was wearing.

Lieutenant Moreau led his new charges up a couple of flights of stairs towards his office. When Henry Bustle commented on the Headquarters building being almost the size of Scotland Yard, the French officer proudly explained that the Gendarmerie Nationale was older than the Metropolitan Police; its history dating back to 1306 during the reign of Philippe le Bel.

"We are responsible gentlemen for policing the smaller towns and rural areas of our country," Moreau explained further, "And of course, assisting visitors from other parts of the world, such as yourselves."

When they reached the French Lieutenant's small office on the third floor, he introduced them to, Arielle Bonnet, a young attractive woman who was dressed as smartly as her senior detective.

"I have asked, Arielle to accompany us to Lyon, because of the implications concerning our dead victim being the wife of your suspect, but there are a number of features in this case I believe you should become acquainted with."

Moreau sat behind his desk after inviting his visitors to also rest their weary legs. Looking down at a file of papers, he then reiterated the contents of a letter directed to the Gendarmerie Nationale and signed by Sir Edmund Henderson, the Commissioner at Scotland Yard.

"Please correct me gentlemen if I miss anything of importance, but according to Sir Edmund's letter, you have a man in custody for having murdered a lady in London, known as Madame Rose Kinley."

"That is correct sir," Rayner confirmed.

"And that this same man has informed you that he once visited the Chateau of Francis Colbert some years before, having met the man in Marseilles whilst serving in the British Navy as a lieutenant."

"Yes."

"And your man, Monsieur Herbert Barratt, had an assignation with Maria Colbert, the wife of Francis Colbert. Again, according to Sir Edmund's information, Colbert discovered his wife in bed with the Englishman and promptly shot the lady to death, before Monsieur Barratt managed to escape."

"So it seems from what Herbert Barratt has told us," Rayner confirmed.

Lieutenant Moreau then sat back and sighed, before asking another question.

"You believe that Monsieur Colbert then sought his revenge on the English lieutenant by travelling to London, where he brutally murdered his wife's former lover's mother and aunt?"

"Again sir, that is what the man has told us."

"And you believe him, monsieur?"

"We have no reason to doubt him."

Moreau then turned to his female assistant and asked her to fetch him the file on, Francis Colbert. Although he spoke in his own language,

Rayner knew enough French to understand. When the lady was absent, her lieutenant explained to his visitors that their suspect was a former Legionnaire who had been kicked out of France's elite company, following allegations of fraud.

"In fact, gentlemen, Monsieur Colbert met his wife Maria, after leaving the Legion and married her. The vineyard that is an ongoing business at the Chateau had been in her family for centuries, and she was the sole proprietor, not her husband."

Both Rayner and Bustle looked surprised and the English Inspector asked his French counterpart, what was the point he was trying to make.

"It is quite simple monsieur. The unfortunate and tragic death of Madame Colbert was recorded as an accidental shooting in the bedroom of the Chateau, but in all cases where the husband in entitled to inherit a vast fortune upon the death of his wife, naturally the circumstances will be viewed with suspicion."

"And was that the case here?" Sergeant Bustle enquired.

Arielle Bonnet then re-entered the room and handed a second file of papers to Moreau, who immediately opened the folder and read from the documents contained within it. He then answered Bustle's query.

"Oui, there was some doubt as to the circumstances in this case, but unfortunately there was insufficient evidence to prove Francis Colbert's version of events was false."

Richard Rayner then stood from his seat and stepped across to lean against a shelf resting above an open fire. The dapper detective from London then, once again, addressed his French counterpart.

"What you are saying monsieur, is that the man Colbert could have easily murdered his wife, not out of rage for having caught her in bed with another man, but for a reason that was more sinister. He had planned the killing in order to inherit the Chateau."

"I am saying Inspector, that there is reason to suspect your man Monsieur Barratt was enticed to the Chateau deliberately by Colbert, and encouraged to sleep with his wife. The intention was always to give the man an excuse to murder the lady. If that was the case, then the motive is clear."

"Have we any evidence to substantiate that claim?"

"No, like you, we are in the dark as they say. But it is a possibility I thought you should know about."

Rayner now wished he'd asked Herbert Barratt during the interview with him back in London, whether Francis Colbert had encouraged him in any way to bed his wife.

"But Lyon awaits gentlemen," Lieutenant Moreau declared, "Arielle will take you to your hotel where you can rest tonight, and we shall start off on our long journey in the morning. I have already sent my Sergeant, Lando Rousseau to Lyon to liaise with Lieutenant Girard down there and he can update us when we arrive."

The hotel selected on their behalf by the French female detective was more than adequate for the two visitors from London. An evening of relaxing and enjoying glasses of French wine, were spent in the hotel bar. Their conversation discussing the new revelations concerning ownership of Colbert's Chateau continued into the early hours, resulting in Henry Bustle sleeping throughout most of the journey to Lyon the following day.

Richard Rayner passed the time by listening to Edvard Moreau's historical anecdotes of most of the cities and regions their carriage passed through, as they continued southwards.

At one stage of the journey, the French Lieutenant explained, "There are two sides of this investigation, which might I suggest, will decide whether Monsieur Colbert will remain in France to stand trial, or be returned to England."

"Whether we find sufficient evidence to prove he murdered his wife," Rayner commented, "Or, whether we can find something that will reveal his guilt regarding the murders committed in London?"

"Exactly, monsieur."

"Please call me Richard."

"Then I am Edvard, Richard."

By the time they reached Lyon, most of the day had passed by and Sergeant Bustle was fully awake to enjoy the wondrous sight of a city built on two rivers, the Rhone, and River Saone. As they approached the city's centre, the architectural wonder of the recently built white stone basilica, Notre Dame de Fourviere, shimmered in the early evening sunshine, reminding Rayner of the Sacre-Coeur basilica in Paris.

The four travellers were met by Edvard Moreau's sergeant, Lando Rousseau and Lieutenant Eamon Girard, the officer in charge of the Gendarmerie Nationale in Lyon. He was a heavily built character of ample girth, coupled with a vivacious manner. A broad grin and protruding eyes were in contrast to the thinly built, solemn and pale faced Sergeant Rousseau.

There was no hesitation in suggesting the travellers rested for the remainder of the night in a local hostel, and Girard insisted they met in his office the following morning. At least they would then be refreshed and better prepared to progress their investigations. All were in agreement and more bottles of French Claret were emptied, although the English visitors remained parsimonious, both wishing to have clear heads for the following day.

"Gentlemen, and of course mademoiselle, welcome to our wondrous city of culture," Lieutenant Girard greeted, sitting at his desk with his small audience facing him, "If we are blessed with an opportunity to show you the historical delights of Lyon a little later, then we shall. But firstly, to business."

Richard Rayner found the robust man to be an amicable fellow, and to date, had been impressed by the French hospitality in general.

"Sergeant Rousseau has been keeping observations on the Chateau in question, together with some of my own men." The lieutenant then nodded towards Moreau's man to continue with the briefing.

"I can confirm that Monsieur Colbert is currently staying at the Chateau, and we have seen him on a couple of occasions in the presence of a young lady, who we have yet to identify."

Each of them was speaking in their own language, and Lieutenant Moreau translated for the benefit of Henry Bustle in particular.

"We also know that our man has firearms inside, and often goes hunting with a rifle," Rousseau continued, "There is also a man servant who resides on the property, and we have observed a number of pruners visiting the vineyard."

"Those are inspectors who scrutinise the growing grapes prior to harvest," Edvard Moreau explained.

"Oui," his sergeant confirmed, "But it is too early for Colbert to harvest his grapes, so I believe the inspection was just interim."

"You see, the best time of the year to harvest the grape is when the weather gets wet and cold," Moreau once again explained, "But it is good to monitor their growth from time to time."

"But, apart from what I have told you, nothing more has happened."

"Are we absolutely positive that the man you have seen there, is Francis Colbert?" Rayner asked.

"Oui, he is known in the district and there can be no doubt, monsieur."

"Have we a warrant to search the property?" the Inspector from Scotland Yard enquired.

"In French law, we do not need any such authority to search in circumstances where an individual is arrested on suspicion of committing a serious crime," Moreau explained.

"Then I suggest gentlemen and lady, we get started without further delay," Rayner said in a determined voice, now feeling the need for more positive action.

After the lieutenant from Calais once interpreted the English man's words they all stood to leave, their next destination being the small town of Saint-Priest.

Chapter Twenty One

The first early morning rays of the sun provided an impressive light display, set against a blue background, the likes of which could only be seen in the South of France. Fingers of changing reds, oranges and golds, reached from horizon to horizon, beckoning to be replicated on an artist's canvas. From a hilltop overlooking the vast vineyard surrounding the Chateau, the town of Saint-Priest could be seen in the distance.

Eamon Girard waited patiently for the men he had deployed to surround the home of Francis Colbert to move into position, watched by Richard Rayner. Both he and his Sergeant had discussed earlier and privately, their realisation that the purpose behind the Scotland Yard detectives' presence there, was being used as a rationale and justification for the Gendarmerie Nationale to investigate further their own suspicions. It had become quite clear that they believed the suspect had committed a murder on French soil; namely that of his wife, Maria Colbert. From previous experience, the English Inspector had always suspected there was a price to pay, or sacrifice to make, when soliciting assistance from another country's law enforcement agencies.

Satisfied that his men were in position, Lieutenant Girard signaled for the small line of horse drawn carriages to follow that which he occupied down a slope, until reaching the edge of the vineyard. Slowly the cortege moved through the narrow breaks dividing the vines, until coming to a halt outside the front of the splendid Chateau.

Armed Gendarmerie seemed to appear from everywhere, their heavy boots slamming down on the gravel beneath their feet, as the officers approached the front door. A butler appeared inside the entrance and was physically pushed to one side, as the group of French Para-Military officers entered a large hallway with a highly polished wooden tiled floor. There were rooms leading off the hallway, and a wide-open spiral staircase leading to the upper tier.

The butler's initial objections were ignored, and numerous pointed rifles were followed by highly trained combatants to various areas of the interior.

Eamon Girard then called out the name of the man in occupation and after a few seconds, Francis Colbert appeared at the top of the staircase. The man was dressed in a silk house coat and could be seen grasping a newly purchased loaded dueling pistol in each hand. The moment the suspected killer had dreaded, since first hearing news of the double murders in Whitechapel having been re-opened, was now reality. And yet, the imaginary course of action he had planned to take in such circumstances; to fight his way back to freedom, was fragile and as determined as a thread of cotton. His dilemma was whether he should surrender peacefully and defend his position with constant denial, or take his own life. He wasn't the kind of individual to favour the latter.

It was the first time Richard Rayner had laid eyes on the man he had travelled all the way from London to apprehend. He stood in the hallway staring back at what he regarded was a figure of a man, whose appearance was similar to that of a swarthy looking gypsy.

Colbert was a tall, well built, powerful looking man, with black curly hair above dark features. His eyes matched the colour of his hair, and a straight narrow nose ran down to a fairly large mouth.

Girard spoke in French when he demanded the occupier released his grip on the firearms.

Colbert stood motionless, staring down at the barrels of two rifles pointing directly at him, smirking in realisation that his instant death would surely follow if he were to disobey. Eventually he shook his head, and slowly placed the weapons on the floor at his feet. It appeared that all of his practice spent previously in firing the pistols, had been a waste.

Girard then informed the suspected man he was being arrested for the murder of his wife, Maria Colbert, and two elderly women in London, England.

The features of the Chateau owner's face suddenly and dramatically changed.

Rayner noticed a feral look come into the man's black eyes; that of a deranged wild-man, which lasted only a fleeting second, and before Colbert began to suddenly burst out laughing aloud. The bizarre sound of his mad laughter entered every room of the Chateau. Remaining where he stood, and glaring down at those who had placed their net of captivity around his world, he threateningly pointed a finger at the lieutenant who was in charge of the raid.

"This is a prank monsieur. I was unaware it was a fete du Travail holiday," Corbett announced, referring to an annual holiday in France to celebrate the end of slavery.

"What in God's name is a fete du Trav... whatever?" Henry Bustle asked, whispering to Richard Rayner. But he was ignored; the Inspector's full concentration was focused on the man he intended taking back to Scotland Yard.

"It is no prank, monsieur," Lieutenant Girard confirmed, before nodding to Sergeant Rousseau to escort the man he had just arrested, back to whichever room he needed to use in order to get dressed.

Whilst they were waiting to place their prisoner into an official carriage, a search of the downstairs rooms was made, with the two English detectives entering the library and commencing an examination of what they could find.

Inspector Rayner was sifting through a number of book shelves, when Edvard Moreau entered and explained, "One of our men has just found this inside the drawer of a small table inside the dining room." He produced a ticket issued in 1860, the same year the murders of the sisters' been committed. According to the print on the ticket, it had been purchased for a stagecoach journey from Dover to London.

Rayner smiled and nodded, before taking possession of the ticket, which was so obviously significant.

"Merci, Edvard," he said, handing the item to Henry Bustle, to keep safe.

After, Moreau had left the library, the Inspector from Scotland Yard remained and continued searching through the shelves, whilst his Sergeant paid attention to a number of drawers contained in a large desk situated inside a bay window.

"I cannot find anything of interest here," Bustle disappointingly said, "Everything is written in French."

But Rayner did not hear the words. His concentration was on a small bundle of papers he had found tucked in between two large books at the end of one particular shelf.

Taking the bundle down, Rayner then stepped across to the desk in the bay window and placed them on the top. Quickly glancing through each copy of La Presse newspaper, he found that each of them contained recent reports of the double murder in Whitechapel, confirming that Scotland Yard had re-opened the case. In some editions, his own name was mentioned and had been uncannily circled with red ink.

The Inspector looked up and remarked, "I think we have sufficient now to take our man back with us Henry."

"Unless of course they find something to suggest he murdered his wife," Bustle replied, pessimistically.

"I doubt that. Their only hope would be that Colbert kept a diary, or they found some correspondence recording what would amount to be a confession to killing his wife in order to inherit this estate."

As the two detectives conversed, there was suddenly a disturbance coming from the floor above them, and a woman's voice was screaming out abuse and various expletives in French. When they ran out into the hallway, they were greeted by the sight of a scantily dressed young girl vociferously objecting to being escorted down the staircase by Arielle Bonnet, Moreau's assistant.

"She is Francis Colbert's fiancée, apparently," Edvard Moreau explained, "And we are taking her with us."

"Where is Colbert now?"

"Secured in the carriage outside. He is less arrogant than when we first arrived."

The three men were joined by Lieutenant Eamon Girard, and Rayner showed them the newspapers he had discovered in the library, all containing reports of the murders he and Bustle were investigating.

"Have you discovered anything that might support your suspicion that Colbert murdered his wife to inherit this estate?"

Both men shook their heads, and Girard admitted, "It is looking more practical that our man goes with you back to London to answer to his foul crimes there, Monsieur Rayner."

When the early morning visitors to the Chateau finally departed, only the butler remained and a peaceful solace enveloped the estate. He wondered whether his master would ever return, and considered looking for another position. It was time to pack his bags and return to Lyon.

Before leaving for England, Lieutenant Moreau offered his services as a translator, for which Richard Rayner was extremely appreciative, and without hesitation, willingly accepted the French officer's invitation to join them. The Englishman had no doubt Edvard Moreau was still hopeful of extracting a confession from Colbert admitting the murder of his wife.

Throughout the channel crossing and eventual stagecoach journey from Dover back to Scotland Yard, the French prisoner remained shackled to Henry Bustle. Lieutenant Moreau frequently expressed his delight at visiting England's capital city for the first time, and was looking forward to seeing the famous Scotland Yard first hand.

As each few miles passed by, Francis Colbert looked more and more desultory and mentally burdened. Their prisoner spoke very few words, and appeared not to understand any of the conversations that were taking place in English, although Rayner remained cautious of what he personally spoke of.

When the small party finally arrived at their destination, Richard Rayner deliberately avoided any meeting with Superintendent Morgan. Instead, he insisted that Henry Bustle introduced Lieutenant Moreau to the senior detective, and updated him on the events that had taken place across the channel.

After escorting Francis Colbert to the interview room contained in the cell block, the Inspector sat alone with the suspect in silence, just staring across the table at the former French Legionnaire. Not once did the suspect look into Rayner's eyes, preferring to just sit there motionless, although obviously uncomfortable. If what he had read in the newspapers about the attributes of this particular Detective Inspector were accurate, he would have to remain extremely diligent and cautious, and wasn't relishing any verbal confrontation with the Scotland Yard Investigator.

Then, after a few minutes, Richard Rayner suddenly blurted out in English, "The Battle of Zaatcha was won by cowards, and I understand that you were there, monsieur?"

Such a statement had the desired effect and Colbert's head sprang up in total surprise. His eyes were filled with fire, as he snarled back at the interviewer, without actually speaking.

"So, as I suspected, you do speak English."

Colbert shook his head and quickly regained his composure. It had been a devious first move by the Inspector, but a successful one.

"Over a thousand Arabs were slaughtered during that battle," Rayner continued, "It was a massacre, according to the records and one which the Legion is not proud of; am I not correct?"

It was futile for Colbert to continue his pretence of not understanding a word spoken in English. He had been found out.

"What the records do not show is that more than two hundred legionnaires also died during that conflict monsieur," the Frenchman stated in perfect English, "And none of them were cowards."

"You were there, I take it?"

Colbert nodded his confirmation.

"Then I must take your word for it. For how long did you serve in the Legion?"

"Too long."

"And I also understand you were discharged following allegations of stealing."

"Why ask me, when you seem to already have the answers."

"Is this the first time you have been to England, monsieur?"

"Oui," the prisoner answered, after some hesitation.

"Then can you tell me why you travelled from Dover to London fifteen years ago," Rayner asked pointedly, before producing the travel ticket found in Colbert's Chateau, and placing it on the table top within sight of the prisoner.

The suspect was surprised, and must have been wondering how he had failed to dispense with such an incriminating item. He held both palms upwards, but not in submission, shaking his head in defiance without verbally answering.

At that moment Henry Bustle entered the room with Edvard Moreau. The Inspector explained they no longer required an interpreter, as the prisoner could speak English.

"Richard," the French Lieutenant said, "I am also here to represent Monsieur Colbert's interests." He then stepped across to the prisoner and leant over him, explaining, "Francis, you are no longer welcome in your own country and if we are forced to take you back to stand trial for the callous murder of Madame Maria Colbert, you will face the Guillotine."

Colbert sat back, looking directly into Moreau's eyes and smiling nervously.

"So, my fellow countryman, there is no escape for you. The English have enough evidence to convict you of the double murders you committed here in London, and for that you will hang, the result being the same; your execution for the vile crimes you have committed."

There was no response from the man and Rayner needed to recover the interview quickly, as he had already felt the possibility of some rapport between himself and Colbert. He suggested that his Sergeant take Lieutenant Moreau for some refreshment, following their lengthy journey that day and Bustle quickly understood his Inspector's requirements.

After the two men had left, leaving the Scotland Yard detective alone once more with the prisoner, the Inspector asked his next question.

"You seem to have taken an interest in the newspaper reports concerning the murders of the two elderly sisters in Whitechapel. I found a number of journals covering the investigation in your library. Do you deny that monsieur?"

"I follow many of the investigations conducted by Scotland Yard."

"And yet it seems strange, the only newspapers I found at your dwelling, contained reports of this particular case. There were no others and a jury would draw the same inferences as I have."

Colbert just shook his head, but Rayner was now beginning to identify glimpses of concern in the Frenchman's eyes.

"This interview is not about trying to get sufficient evidence from you for a conviction monsieur," the Inspector explained, "We already have that. I am appealing to you for the truth." He then continued to introduce the circumstances of how Colbert had first met Herbert Barratt, and had taken him back to his Chateau outside Saint-Priest.

"Whether or not you killed your wife because you intended to claim the inheritance of her estate, is not important to me. I actually believe that you came to London and murdered Barratt's mother and aunt as an act of sheer revenge."

"Non, you are wrong Inspector."

"Then you tell me; why did you murder those defenceless women? Such atrocities are not what you would expect from a former Legionnaire."

Colbert leaned forward and grasped both hands on the table top. His eyes were filled with self-pity, but his voice sounded defiant.

"I did not act out of revenge. I am not that kind of person." He paused and a slight grin came on his face, before continuing, "Monsieur Barratt was a pathetic creature who only took advantage of my wife, because I encouraged him. You have to believe that. At the time, the Estate was suffering badly. The two years before, we had little harvest and were facing ruination. Your Englishman, Barratt, boasted of his mother and aunt having a small fortune hidden away in their shop in Whitechapel. He even told me where the shop was."

Now it was, Richard Rayner who sat back to take stock of what had just been said, before suggesting, "So, you did murder your wife because you were chasing the inheritance?" It was a risky deviation from the ongoing conversation regarding the atrocities committed in London, but the Inspector now believed the man's psychological intentions against his wife were linked to the murders of the two sisters'.

"I will not admit to the death of my wife to the Gendarmerie monsieur, but yes, I visited those women in London to steal from them and not out of revenge. At the time, I was desperate."

"How did you gain access into their shop and living quarters?"

"I saw Herbert Barratt enter the shop with another man and they seemed to stay inside for hours. The man who was with him left before Barratt did, and as soon as that worthless, miserable toad came out of the shop and disappeared, I knocked on the front door. It was opened by one of the women. She thought at first I was the Englishman returning, but when she saw me, she tried to slam the door closed, but I managed to force my way in."

"What time was this?"

"I cannot remember. It was very late. Perhaps two or three o'clock in the morning, but all I wanted was their money, but they resisted. I tried to frighten them but they were stubborn, until I just lost control and you know the rest."

"What weapon did you use?"

"My walking stick, which I had with me. It had a metal handle."

"Why did you not search the room?"

"I did, but was careful not to disturb anything. I heard some noise outside the front of the shop and decided to leave. I had gone all that way and killed two women, without finding any fortune, which according to the lying Herbert Barratt, should have been there. I even searched upstairs, but there was nothing. It was madness; lunacy."

"It was murder monsieur for which you will sacrifice your life."

After clearing up a few other issues with Colbert, Rayner stood and called for an officer to take him to the cells.

As he was leaving, the prisoner turned and asked, "What will happen to me now, monsieur?"

"You will be hanged monsieur, unfortunately, only once for three foul murders."

Epilogue

The severe winter of 1875 had finally passed on, leaving in its wake, many scars on people's memories. The number of newly filled graves, mostly of poor souls and wretched infants who hadn't survived the prolonged freezing conditions on London's streets, had increased dramatically. And whether or not lessons had been learned, would remain unanswered until the next Arctic blast was experienced.

One success story reported in the newspapers, was the capture of two killers; one a French citizen who had remained hidden in his safe haven for the past fifteen years. The other, a misfortunate street beggar with an unbalanced mind and who, like so many other homeless and destitute beings, had suffered miserably from a severe drink addiction. An outcast who, as a result of his own affliction, had been propelled towards ending his life on the gallows.

Richard Rayner had once again been given hero status, and although such accolades were never treated seriously by Scotland Yard's most famous detective, his aptitude for delving successfully into historical cases was strengthened with each additional case allocated to him and his trusted Sergeant, Henry Bustle.

Of course, Superintendent Frederick Morgan had claimed the success of the outstanding achievement was shared with his Detective Department, but everyone knew and accepted who it had been to bring about such accolades.

There were no celebrations following the convictions of Francis Colbert and Herbert Barratt. Both men were confined in Pentonville Prison until the dates of their appointments with the hangman finally arrived.

Surprisingly, the London Gazette reported that the Frenchman had screamed out for mercy and had violently resisted prison officers, as he was escorted in shackles from the condemned cell to his place of execution.

Herbert Barratt on the other hand, had made the same short walk with a straight back and wry smile on his face, saying very little before standing on the trap door with the noose around his neck.

"I suppose Colbert's young son will inherit his mother's estate near Saint-Priest," Sergeant Bustle assumed, as both detectives walked away from the confines of Pentonville Prison, following the executions.

"The boy will do just that Henry, according to Edvard Moreau."

The couple continued their walk, hoping to soon see a cabbie approaching.

"I don't know why we have to bear witness to these executions, Inspector," Sergeant Bustle then protested, looking a little downhearted, "It's something I never look forward to."

"I agree Henry," answered Rayner, "But it's part of our job in the same way as we try and seek out the perpetrators of the murders they commit."

"But why do they allow members of the public to also witness the same proceedings? It's barbaric."

"You are absolutely correct and it's time we stopped those who attend for ghoulish reasons," the Inspector agreed.

"Perhaps, one day we will sir."

"Perhaps one day Henry, there will be no more so called lawful executions."

There was a cloudless sky up above, and the Sun's rays reflected off the white structure of the impressive Baroque styled building of Christ Church in Commercial Street, Tower Hamlets. Its tall spire stood proud, like a pointing finger against a blue open sky, and there was an atmosphere of celebration and joy, as the bells melodiously rang out. Richard Bridge's eighteenth-century magnificent organ could be heard in full flow, penetrating the immediate area from within the church.

The tall, thin figure of Willie Collins stood nervously at the side of Jack Robinson, and both the Bridegroom and Best Man glanced at each other apprehensively, as they heard the rustle of the bride's skirts coming along the aisle.

"You have the ring?" Jack mimed to his friend, who answered with a nod of his head and pat of a hand on top of his jacket pocket.

The Groom's mother sat directly behind her son, listening to every word and instantly felt relieved when young Willie confirmed that he hadn't forgotten the most important task allocated to him.

Lizzie Donogue looked stunning as she reached her future husband's side, and the young couple had to wait facing the parson, until Mendelssohn's Wedding March had been concluded.

Both Richard Rayner and Henry Bustle sat in pews at the very back of the church, with Nellie Bustle sitting next to her husband, already tearful. Being the devoted husband he was, the Sergeant handed a clean white handkerchief to his lady, which had only been ironed that same morning.

Upon enquiring, the Inspector had been told by his most trusted colleague, that the four little Bustles' had been left in the care of a neighbour, and Rayner was delighted to hear it.

Frederick Morgan was also there, glancing around the church with his usual eye of righteousness, as if searching through the other members of the congregation for his next arrest.

"He seems more tense than the Bridegroom," the Sergeant whispered, to which the Inspector chuckled.

Following the ceremony, they all followed Jack Robinson from the church, as he led his new wife out into the bright sunshine, beneath an archway of wooden batons held up by many of his colleagues from Scotland Yard. A line of horse drawn carriages also stood outside the front of the church, waiting to take the newly-weds off to their reception at The Plume of Feathers in North Street. It had been a fitting end to a turbulent period in young Jack's life. A period which had begun with an opportunity to work alongside the most revered detective at Scotland Yard, only to be interrupted by the most violent and threatening episode he had experienced in his life thus far.

Neither Rayner nor Bustle heard the approaching footsteps from behind them.

"Well now, the new Mrs. Robinson and that bairn of theirs will keep young Jack busy for a time," Frederick Morgan suggested.

"I don't think he'll mind that Superintendent," the Inspector replied with a smile.

"Not wanting to be the man who throws cold water on such a joyful event Inspector," the Superintendent continued, "But something has come up and the Commissioner requires our presence back at Scotland Yard."

Both Rayner and his Sergeant looked suddenly dejected, realising they would not be able to toast the newly weds health at The Plume of Feathers, after all.

"How old is this one?" the Sergeant enquired.

"Don't be insolent Bustle."

"I'll have to go and speak with the wife. She's going to love you, Superintendent."

Richard Rayner chuckled to himself, knowing that very soon there would be a vociferous outburst of objection coming from Nellie Bustle, which was the only reason the Superintendent was hurrying away to summon a cab.

If you enjoyed reading this book, we recommend another series written by the same author:

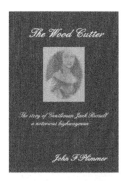

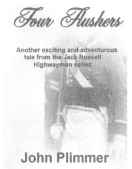

About the Author

John F Plimmer retired from the West Midlands force as a prominent high-profile detective following a thirty one year illustrious career in which he was responsible for the investigation of more than 30 murder inquiries, all of which were detected successfully.

During a four-year period working for the Regional Crime Squad and Security Forces, Plimmer participated in the introduction of professional training and support for covert agents in the West Midlands and other parts of the country. His experience in dealing with undercover operations linked him with overseas agents in Holland, Belgium, Spain, Morocco and Germany.

Following his retirement, he lectured in Law at Birmingham University and became a columnist and feature writer for The Sunday Mercury and Birmingham Evening Mail. Today he frequently participates in discussions and interviews on police and legal subjects on both television and radio.

His television work has included working as a script consultant on popular programmes such as Dalziel and Pascoe and Cracker.

His published works include a number of Home Office Blue Papers on Serious Crime Management and Covert Police Handling. He is the author of a number of published books which include 'In the Footsteps of the Whitechapel Murders' (The Book Guild); Inside Track; Running with the Devil; The Whitechapel Murders and Brickbats & Tutus (House of Stratus).

He is a dedicated reader of Louis L'Amour often giving L'Amour's work as the reason for spending years researching the old pioneering west.

His western novels include 'The Invisible Gun' 'Apache Justice' and 'The Butte Conspiracy'. His book, 'The Cutting Edge' is a partially factual account of the biggest bank hoist ever committed in the history of the United Kingdom. The same work is the first of a series featuring Dan Mitchell, a British agent working for the Deep Cover Agency of the Foreign Office.

Other published books written by John Plimmer include:

Dan Mitchell series:

Cutting Edge
Red Mist
The Food Mountain
The Neutron Claw
Chinese Extraction
Wrangel Island
Justice Casee

Western Triology:

Tatanka Jake
Apache Justice
The Butte Conspiracy

Highwayman Series
In the Footsteps of the Highwaymen
The Wood Cutter
The Return
Four Flushers

Inside Track
Running with the Devil
In the Footsteps of Capone
The World's most Notorious Serial Killers
In the Footsteps of the Whitechapel Murders
Fallen Paragons – The story of the West Midlands Serious Crime Squad
Brickbats & Tutus
Backstreet Urchins
George's War
Hilda's War
The Victorian Detective's Case Review
A Farthing for a Life

Printed in Great Britain
by Amazon ·

83986982R00140